HATING HEIDI FOSTER

JEFFREY BLOUNT

Hating Heidi Foster
Copyright © 2012
By Jeffrey Blount

Alluvion Press
P.O. Box 40144
Washington, DC 20016

This is a work of fiction. All of the characters, organizations, and events portrayed in this novel are either products of the author's imagination or are used fictitiously.

First Edition

ISBN 978-0-9857627-0-4

HATING HEIDI FOSTER

A Novel

JEFFREY BLOUNT

For

Julia Blount and Emily Kelin

Author's Note

I WISH TO ACKNOWLEDGE my wife, Jeanne Meserve, for her enduring love and support. I would like to thank my readers. A very special note of appreciation to Rachel Mitnick. Also, Joy Lerner, Steve Kelin, Kathy Meserve, Joe Cortina, David Hanson, Demetrea Triantafilledes, and Susie Meserve. Big thanks to Malaga Baldi for her encouragement and sage advice. And to Edward and Doris Blount for their continued guidance and faith.

ONE

I HAVE NEVER BEEN VERY GOOD with faces. It often took many meetings and surreptitious glances before I was able to rightfully place those freckles, that wide grin, the plucked brows or to place a face to a name. Even after someone had been in my life for years, I could easily fail to conjure up that person's face if they dropped out of my world for any significant amount of time. This flaw of mine has always been a part of me, but before this moment it had never seemed insurmountable. There had always been time for some facial reconnections, but the stakes had never been this high before. What to do with this chink in my armor now that there was a truly important face that needed remembering? What to do?

That's what I found myself thinking as I looked past my grandfather at the water's edge to Mummy, who was standing waist deep in the slow-moving river. Her arms were wrapped around her body tightly, her shoulders rising and falling with her sobs. Just seconds before, she'd completed the ceremonial task that would mark the end of my father's life. With her friend Lil standing on the riverbank singing "Amazing Grace", she'd waded in and stopped with her back to all of us. I tried to imagine what she was thinking, feeling, or whispering to him. But that hurt too much, so I tried to concentrate only on Lil's singing. And when that didn't work, I closed my eyes and tried to lose myself in my grandmother's arms, which were wrapped tightly around me. But I could feel her against my back, her body quivering with a mother's grief for her son. There could be no peace for me there. So, I opened my eyes and returned my gaze to Mummy just as her arms began to rise. She'd opened the urn and I could see rose petals spreading out on the water on either side of her. With Lil still in full song and the petals floating away along with Daddy's ashes, I felt something go very wrong inside. I hated.

Mummy blew a kiss to the sky. Lil finished and we all stood still in the tender quiet and waited until Mummy finished crying and came to my grandfather who wrapped her in his arms. I heard her soft sigh and call for help as he pulled her close. "Oh, Daddy," was all she said, but I knew that she was really asking him, "What do I do? And how will I live?"

It's an unspoken language between father and daughter. I could never complete a thoughtful or needy question before the smile turned up on my father's face telling me that he already understood.

Mummy was still a daddy's girl. The way Grandpa rocked her told me that after all the years of living apart, he still understood. But my relationship with my father was now ashes on the river and I felt myself becoming jealous of Mummy, because as of that day, I would never be a daddy's girl again.

TWO

It's Heidi Foster that I hated. She had become the absolute bane of my existence. Because she was too stupid to think straight, I no longer had a father. Because she was so mentally challenged, I would never again hear him whisper "Daddy loves you" in my ear while I pretended to be asleep. Because of Heidi Foster, Mummy cried every morning and every night and zombied her way through the days. Because of Heidi Foster, I felt lost in the darkest room in the darkest house in the world.

It was the summer of 2003. It was supposed to be my time in the sun. I'd turned fourteen that past spring and graduated from middle school. I spent the summer wondering and dreaming about high school. It was such a big deal. A different campus, forty new kids, new academic challenges, and volleyball. Daddy always laughed whenever anyone mentioned my name in relation to volleyball. Whenever anyone wondered out loud what was so funny about me playing a sport, Mummy would laugh as well and then feel compelled to retell what was by now her favorite family tale.

As she tells the story, Mummy was not at all surprised. When I was a newborn, she walked into my bedroom with me for the first time, preparing to place me in the bassinet; lying on the little mattress was a tennis racquet. She says she just started to laugh.

She wasn't surprised because back in high school, Daddy had lettered in football and baseball. He was so good at those that he didn't even mind telling the story of how he was cut while trying out for the basketball team. The basketball coach had said to him, "Son, you play football well. Play football, son." Not one to sit still, Daddy picked up karate during basketball season in middle school and by the time he graduated from high school, he'd competed up and down the East Coast and was very proud of the fact that he never came home from a tournament without a trophy. Not all of them were for first place, but he never came home empty handed. He walked off a football field for the last time after his senior season in college.

She wasn't surprised because throughout her pregnancy, he talked to her tummy about sports. He read the box scores and discussed player trades and coach firings. He called me — at this point unnamed — Sport.

She wasn't surprised, but she still laughed to see the racquet where I was supposed to sleep.

"Baby," she asked him, "don't you think you're pushing a little bit too early?"

She says he stood there a little embarrassed, his hands locked behind him, his feet shuffling, and his head down like a little boy who knows he did wrong but couldn't help himself.

"Well, why not a football?" she asked him. "You don't play tennis."

"There's no opportunity for her to play pro football."

"Oh, Baby. You're just gone."

She says he just stood there.

"She's going to have a mind of her own, you know."

She says he just stood there.

She handed him the racquet and laid me down to sleep.

Daddy so loved everything about being an athlete and he said he'd always dreamed of having a little jock — girl or boy. But after all the tennis racquets and tennis balls hung from the ceiling in my playroom, he ended up with his worst nightmare: me, the ultimate girly-girl. I despised sports and he would just laugh and shake his head, not understanding how he could have fathered a child like me. Usually, he blamed it all on Mummy and she accepted with pride. But he was my daddy, which meant he put all of that aside and sat on the floor and played girly-girl games with me, everything from dressing up dolls to playing house. One board game called Pretty, Pretty Princess required each player to acquire earrings, a necklace, and rings. Daddy wore his with pride and never backed down from the picture Mummy took of him and then placed on the fridge where every visitor could see it. He did all of that stuff with me because he loved me more than sports. But then I hit middle school where you were required to play sports because athletics supposedly made for a more well-rounded student. He soon found that he hadn't failed after all. I fell in love with volleyball and he made it to almost every game. He looked so proud in the stands and I loved being able to bring that "I just can't believe it" smile to his face. I made JV this year in try-outs before the beginning of school. Daddy and Mummy were planning on being at the first game. But now that can't be and because of Heidi Foster, I knew there would always be an empty spot in the bleachers for me.

Everything had been set for me to blow into the high school at Washington, DC's prestigious Hawthorne Day School and set the world on fire. Now on the first day of classes, I struggled to find a reason to even show up. Mummy sat beside me in the car and we looked up at Heidi, who was standing at the top of the stairs by the school's entrance. She was getting a hug from the principal. Why was he hugging her? She was crying. What was she so upset about? She had her damned life, didn't she? She had her father, didn't she? I turned and looked at Mummy. Her face reflected what I thought and I knew she understood. But I had to go to school, didn't I?

It took everything I had to get out of that car and walk towards the school's entrance. By the time I was halfway to the stairs, the vice-principal and a teacher had joined in the Heidi support group. And then my heart stopped when I saw Ellie come out of the building and swallow Heidi in the biggest hug imaginable. What could she possibly have left for me, I wondered?

That's when the tears started and I couldn't control them at all. I turned and looked at Mummy who was also crying. This was so hard. As I started up the staircase, I saw Ellie walk Heidi into the school. Mr. Barr, the principal, was waiting at the top. He began to move towards me, but I moved away without even really planning to. I just couldn't go near him.

"Mae," he called to me.

But I just cried and continued to move away. "You stay away from me!" I heard myself yell. "She took my father and you hug her for it!"

"But, Mae, surely you understand why she needs comforting too."

"I don't understand anything anymore," I shouted and ran away through the front doors.

When I came through the doors into the lobby, it was as if I had done so without any pants. Everyone stared. I had been a part of this school community since kindergarten, but all of a sudden it was as if I was the new kid. Everyone acted as if they didn't know me anymore. I was too upset to think about it clearly because the truth was I didn't know me anymore either. I had been fundamentally changed inside and maybe it showed all over my face.

By now, they were all there with her — Ellie, Zoe, Charlotte, Paige, Maria, and Carol. They were taking turns hugging her, brushing her hair, wiping her tears, and trying to cheer her up. I stood there in the middle of the lobby with everyone staring at me except the people I cared about the most.

Finally, Ellie saw me and she came running toward me, but I found myself shaking my head and backing away. As she got closer, I just turned and ran back through the doors and down the stairs. I don't know where I was planning on going. I just couldn't stay there anymore. But as I got down the stairs, I realized that Mummy was still there. The car door was open already and I fell in. We didn't speak. There was no need to. I closed the door and we cried all the way home.

When we got home, we climbed into my parents' bed. I laid my head on Mummy's chest and quickly gave into my exhaustion and fell asleep.

When I awoke, our backs were turned toward one another. I listened to Mummy's labored breathing. I knew she was dreaming bad dreams because I was having them too. For a while, I lay there sighing, twisting, turning, pulling my knees up to my chest, stretching out my legs, rolling over, and sighing some more. I was just uncomfortable and out of sorts. I felt weakened by some kind of invisible weight. Sometimes I felt as if I could barely get out of bed and put one foot in front of the other. I was totally out of balance. I had expected the psychological struggle, because you always hear about people having emotional trouble dealing with their grief. But the physical side effects were big news to me.

When it got to the point that I was afraid of waking Mummy, I forced myself to get out of bed and go to my own room. I just walked around in circles looking at the posters on my wall like they were museum pieces I was seeing for the first time. There were Star Wars posters and Lord of the Rings posters: Frodo and Sam with the big evil eye hovering above them. Daddy was crazy about Lord of the Rings. We stood in long lines together for hours in the cold just to get the perfect seat in the perfect theatre. We had so much fun.

Thinking of Daddy like that made me feel a little better, but then just as quickly I felt anxious and intensely fearful about my future. Where did that come from? It kept happening right out of the blue. Peace destroyed by terrible hurt and fear, which was just how it had been the moment I answered the door three weeks before and the soft-spoken officer asked if my mother was home.

She was in the kitchen on the telephone trying to reach Daddy's cell. He was late and she'd finished cooking dinner because he'd called to tell her he was on the way home. Just before the officer arrived, she had been dialing and dialing and muttering about why he didn't call to say something had changed.

When the officer walked into the kitchen behind me, I was already crying and he didn't waste any time. Maybe he'd had to do this before and he knew that drawing things out only made it more painful. So he just said, "Mrs. McBride?"

Mummy nodded and her eyes began to fill.

"I'm sorry," he said. "Your husband has died."

Mummy began to cry and I fell into her arms.

I knew for sure then that he had done this before. He was gentle but very businesslike. Maybe he knew that he could never really console either of us. In the end, I appreciated his manner. He needed to let us know and we needed him to leave so that we could begin to understand how quickly and drastically our lives had changed. So he said what he had to say, telling us briskly about the fire and Daddy's part in it. He handed her his card and told her to call him if she had any questions.

Mummy stood there, her face open and expecting, but the officer just said, "That's all I have now, ma'am. I'll see myself out."

The dinner on the table that was already cold remained there until the wee hours of the morning when Mummy's parents arrived from Boston.

While I was staring at Frodo Baggins, but thinking of everything else, my computer produced a familiar tone, letting me know that the door had opened on my instant messaging account. A buddy was online. All of my buddies were at school taking care of Heidi, so I knew it could only be Daddy's mother. It was so cute that Gran Gran, who hated computers, got an AOL account just so she could stay in close contact with me. I loved her for it.

Gran Gran: Sweetie, you home?

VballQueen: How did you know? I'm supposed to be in school.

Gran Gran: Well, it was your first day and I just had this feeling come over me. I felt like you needed me.

VballQueen: Well, your intuition is still good.

Gran Gran: How is your mummy?

VballQueen: Sleeping. It was a tough morning for us.

Gran Gran: I'm sure. You should be sleeping too, you know. Every chance you get.

VballQueen: I do in spurts, but I've been having bad dreams.

Gran Gran: Well, I'm not surprised by that.

VballQueen: Actually, it's just one dream. And truthfully, I'm afraid to even go to sleep.

Gran Gran: Do you want to tell me about it? Maybe it will help to tell someone.

VballQueen: Ok. If you think so. Here goes… It is so hot when I realize that I'm the one in the closet. And the house is burning. I hear a lamp crash because an end table has burned away from beneath it. The big paintings fall from the walls and the glass breaks. The flame is burning, crackling, and popping. I can tell the fire is getting closer to the closet, because I am getting hotter. I start to sweat and then it gets so hot that it begins to hurt, like someone is pinching and twisting your skin all over your body. And I have never been so scared. I never knew this kind of fear even existed. But I keep thinking he will come, Gran Gran. But he doesn't. He just doesn't come for me. And it starts to hurt so much that I begin to scream in pain. And then I wake up breathing hard, sweating, and I cannot hold back my tears or my anger.

Gran Gran: Sweetie, that sounds so terrible. I wish I could be there. I wish I could sit by your bed and rub your back and whisper that everything will be all right. It just breaks my heart to hear this.

VballQueen: I'm sorry.

Gran Gran: Oh, don't apologize. Please. Would you do something for me?

VballQueen: Yes, of course.

Gran Gran: Go find a phone and call me. I think we need to hear each other's voices.

VballQueen: K.

So I snuck back into my parents' bedroom, where Mummy still lay sleeping. I took the phone from Daddy's side of the bed and returned to my room. I dialed and Gran Gran picked up on the first ring and I just started bawling.

"There had to be that moment when he knew what he was risking. When he could have turned back. Why did he put Heidi before me, Gran Gran? Didn't he think about the fact that he would be leaving Mummy and me alone? Me without a father! How could he do this to me?"

"Oh, Mae, I know he didn't mean to leave you. I think he wanted to do the right thing and I know he hoped that he would make it out safely back to all of us."

"But why would he even try? Why couldn't he wait like everyone else for the firefighters? Why did he have to try to be a hero? Why did he choose Heidi over me?"

"I don't know why he tried or why he wouldn't wait and I don't think he had being a hero on his mind. You and I both know him better than that. And I know that he loved Heidi. You've been best friends since you were six. Eight years of her sleeping over, having meals, movies, camping. All of the stuff you guys did. But even with that I just have a feeling that whatever made him act is bigger than Heidi. I wish I knew what, but I don't think we will ever know that now. Not until we see him on the other side."

"I just don't know. How do you live with the wondering why? Sometimes I get so mad at him. So mad."

"I understand."

"So you get mad at him too?"

"No, Sweetie. I don't."

"Why not?"

"I understand why you do. I really do. Maybe for me and Pop Pop it has something to do with the fact that we had him for forty-six years. You had him for only fourteen. We've talked about it. We don't feel cheated really. We feel like we had a good life with him and he gave us so much joy and his memory will continue to do that."

"How is Pop Pop?"

"He is doing well. He takes care of me. He hugs me and hugs me and hugs me whenever I need it."

"Do you hug him when he needs it?"

"Yes, ma'am. I surely do. The all-day-long kind."

"Who hugs my daddy? He burned to death. He had to be hurting so badly. There was no one there for him."

Now Gran Gran began to cry and I felt bad for making that happen. I just held the phone to my ear and listened. Every now and then I told her that I loved her.

"I'm sorry, Gran Gran," I finally said. "I just miss him so. And I feel so much like I'm losing him. It's only been three weeks and I can't see him when I think of him and I feel as if I've even forgotten the tone of his voice."

"Well, you have to do what I've been doing. I have all these tapes from Christmases and anniversaries and other visits that you guys made here. I just watch and listen and feel him. I've put new pictures in the bedroom. They help to keep him with us. I know he had hours and hours of tape of your family. Now might be a good time to look at them."

"I can't do that."

She sounded surprised. "Why not?"

"Mummy won't allow it. I thought about playing back the tape of us on the rafting trip we took. He was really funny in it and it shows a lot of him. A lot of the family tapes have Mummy and me on them, but not him because he was doing all the videotaping. Sometimes, I can watch an entire tape and never see him. Especially, when I was little, before I started taking the camera away from him and videotaping him instead. But Mummy says she couldn't take that just yet and she doesn't want to walk into a room and hear me listening either. So, I can't do that."

"Well, we all grieve differently. Maybe when she's not at home sometimes and you keep it to yourself."

"Gran Gran. Are you telling me to disobey my mother? You, the ultimate 'you must do what your parents say' person."

I had to laugh and so did she.

"Yes, I am. Just this time. Because you have to grieve in the way you need to as well. Your mummy would understand that if she didn't have such a huge cloud of pain around her now. I love your mummy as if she were my own and she brought such joy to my son and for that I will always love her. Always! But I want to help you take care of yourself as well. Wait until she's not home, ok?"

"Ok and thanks, Gran Gran. I'm kind of tired again. I think I'm going to go stretch out next to Mummy, even if it's only to hear her breathe."

"I love you, Mae McBride. I truly do."

"I love you too, Gran Gran. I truly do."

But before I went to Mummy, I went downstairs to the kitchen and pushed the answer button on the phone. It was Daddy's voice. "Hello...Leave a message for Eddie, Renata or Mae and we'll get back to you as soon as possible...bye." "Bye to you too, Daddy," I thought.

I lay down beside Mummy and thought of the incredible loss in her heart. He was the man in our lives and for me he was truly larger than life. In his hands, the sun was only a flame atop a votive candle that he would set at my bedside as a special nightlight. The Eiffel Tower was just a wonderfully ornate paperweight left to hold down the little notes of fatherly pride he would leave on my desk. And the greatest of the pyramids was a simple top, which he would turn over and spin, just to make me laugh.

THREE

A MONTH LATER MY LIFE SEEMED to be settling down, even if it was doing so into something that felt very much apart from me. Something I seemed to have no control over. Almost always, I acted in ways that surprised me and by the time I had figured out why, I'd already done something else unexpected. For instance, never in my life had I been able to be really rude to anyone. It just wasn't in me. Mummy and Daddy never allowed it. But now, I seemed to be rude all the time. And though I knew I was about to be rude, in fact I could feel it coming on like just before you're about to throw up, I didn't have the capacity to stop it. Kids would come up to me to express sympathy and I would look through them as if they were glass and say nothing or turn and walk the other way. By now, my old friends were busy giving up on me. When they tried to speak to me, I called them "Heidi lovers" and spit on the floor by their feet. Some of them cried. Others stood still, completely befuddled by the girl they thought they knew. Several, like Maria, Ellie, and Charlotte, tried several times.

But eventually, they retired to watching from a distance, hoping to see the old me if only for a second or two. But the old me could not exist at Hawthorne Day School.

Back on the second day of school, I sat crying in the car with Mummy.

"We both have to be strong," she said. "We have to live, don't we?"

"I guess," I replied, watching Mr. Barr greet students at the door. I made up my mind not to speak to him. How could I ever after the fuss he made over Heidi Foster?

I kissed Mummy and stepped out of the car. I made my way up the opposite side of the staircase from Mr. Barr and he did not try to talk to me. I turned around to wave to Mummy, but she was gone. I think she didn't want to give me the opportunity to run again. "We have to live, don't we?" she'd said.

So I walked into my school and felt terrible. I knew that all of my classmates liked Heidi. She was very popular but not in the negative sense. A good kid who was so peaceful that everyone just felt good in her presence. And now they felt sorry for her. I couldn't feel sorry for her. I still hated her and so I could not tolerate anyone who could muster one iota of sympathy for her. I felt the sympathy should have been all mine. So I had to put the old me away to survive. I had to shut them all out, because they were all now in the enemy camp. It was Heidi Foster or Mae McBride. No sitting on the fence allowed.

Eventually, I found myself alone. Not ostracized. Just alone. I don't think anyone hated me. They just couldn't be comfortable around me, especially if I were in the vicinity of one of my old buddies. Then everyone, including teachers, became very uncomfortable. It was like some bad toxin was in the air that forced everyone to run for the nearest exit of the building and the mind. They just backed away and the more they did, the more I liked it. I didn't want anyone to be nice to me. I didn't want anyone to steal or calm my hatred. My jaws would hurt at the end of the day from walking around with this tense and angry look on my face. For the first time in my life, I had a nickname. "The Tragic One."

"HA!" was Mummy's reaction to my new call sign. Then she roared with laughter and I was simply stunned. So stunned that I literally forgot to laugh with her. Mummy hadn't really smiled since Daddy died. Maybe the corners of her mouth had turned up a little in a forced attempt to show some joy, but it never grew into her full smile and then into a head-tossed-back, free-for-all moment of laughter. But now it had and she'd caught me completely by surprise.

"I think," she said when she'd calmed down, "that this nickname would have been perfect for you before any of this happened."

I dove into her arms and held on for dear life. I guess I just wanted to feel what she was feeling. I wanted to know the release of laughter, but I only managed a smile. But at least it was a legitimate one and mostly due to the fact that she was coming back to life.

"I suppose you're right," I replied.

"Suppose! You, always the drama queen, playing the wounded one knowing that your daddy would come and fix you up until your next tragedy. Who gave you this name? I want to say thanks."

She was still laughing.

"I don't know. I just started hearing it along the way."

"Just too much," she said, turning and walking up the stairs still laughing. "You know Daddy would have loved this."

After this conversation, I began to feel strangely attached to my new nickname. And Mummy would begin to use it as my pet name.

"Oh Tragic One, would you mind switching the laundry to the dryer?"

"Come on, Tragic One. We'll be late."

In due time, I changed my screen name to that on my AOL account. Gran Gran didn't get the joke.

Gran Gran: What's this new name?

The Tragic One: It's what they call me at school.

Gran Gran: Well, that's not very nice.

The Tragic One: It's OK, really. And it made Mummy laugh for the first time since Daddy died.

Gran Gran: She thinks it fits?

The Tragic One: She does and she said Daddy would have too.

Gran Gran: Ok, if you guys say so. But what does it mean to the other kids?

The Tragic One: They think I've gone off the deep end never to come back.

Gran Gran: You still having trouble forgiving?

The Tragic One: That's an understatement!

Gran Gran: You have to let go, Sweetie. This is going to eat you up inside.

The Tragic One: I know, but I can't. When I see their faces. When I see Heidi's face. I just grow all hard inside. Then I just retreat. The funny thing is that my grades have gotten better. Wouldn't you expect the opposite?

Gran Gran: Yes, I've been worried about that actually. You have always been such a wonderful student.

The Tragic One: Well, studying is a solitary thing and I'm into all things solitary. Especially if it takes my mind away to other places and things. Even so, teachers keep trying to talk me into visiting them during my free period. You know, just to talk. Like they think they can fix me or something. Like they can erase what's happened.

Gran Gran: They just want to help, Baby. They just want to help.

The Tragic One: Oh, Gran Gran, that's what Mummy used to call him all the time you know.

Gran Gran: Your dad?

The Tragic One: Yes. Mummy always said, "Baby, I love you." Or "Baby, could you help me in here?" Or "Baby, turn off the football and come to bed." I always loved how that sounded. I miss it so much.

Gran Gran: Now that you mention it, I can hear her myself.

The Tragic One: Sweet!

Gran Gran: Oh, Mae. Pop Pop just came in the room. He says hello and asks if he can come to a volleyball game.

The Tragic One: Oh, I don't think he'd want to. I'm not starting anymore.

Gran Gran: What happened?

The Tragic One: It's not something solitary.

Gran Gran: Oh.

The Tragic One: But tell him not to worry. I'll get it back.

Gran Gran: I hope so, Sweetie. I hope so.

The Tragic One: Well, give Pop Pop a big hug for me and I will see you soon.

Gran Gran: Ok, Tragic One. You are in my prayers always.

The Tragic One: I love you truly.

Gran Gran: I love you truly. I do!

The next day, as I was spraying volleyballs all over the gym, I laughed and cringed at the thought of Pop Pop sitting in the stands watching me make a fool out of myself. I just couldn't concentrate. When I tried to serve, I'd toss the ball into the air and before it reached its apex, my mind would have wandered off. I'd be thinking about what that group over there might be saying about me and I'd be cursing them for it when I remembered that I'd tossed the ball. Then, I would react and start my swing, which would inevitably be late or not straight on and the ball would fly off into whatever direction. The coach would just shake her head and leave me on the bench. I'd come to her with all of this hype from the middle school coach and now, no matter how badly we might be beating someone, I couldn't get off the bench. She said she had sympathy for me, but she also wanted to win games and keep her job. I just shrugged her off, but I was all messed up inside.

I remembered two games in particular from middle school. During the first one, I made my first spike. I'm only five feet eight inches tall, but I had surprised the coach and my teammates by playing around in practice and spiking the ball. So, she started me on the front line in the hopes that I could smack down a couple before I rotated into the backcourt. I did just that on the first point. It was Ellie who set me up and I smacked it down. There was a big roar from the mostly parent crowd and I saw Daddy standing with his hands on his hips, he head cocked to one side and this smirk/smile on his face that said *you stop showing off.* I smiled back at him and did it three more times.

On the way home, he said. "Hey, you've got some serious hops, young lady." I said thank you and I was full of pride and to this day it remains the most important compliment ever given to me.

In the next-to-last game of my eighth grade season, I almost single-handedly won the final game of a match. I served twelve straight winning points with five of them being clean winners. I brought us back and served out the match. That, like Daddy being alive, all seemed like a dream or a good book about somebody else's life that I'd read long ago.

By the end of practice, I was sitting off to the side staring at everybody else. The coach called us all in, but I didn't move and she didn't make the extra effort to call me over. After a small chat and a few peppy cheers, which I used to help lead, the team jogged to the locker room. I just sat there waiting for something and nothing.

A few minutes went by before I heard the ball bouncing towards me. It came along with one of the new girls on the team. Her name was Alexandra Carr and she was, at six feet two inches, the tallest girl on the team. She was very talented and a witch to boot. She wore a pendant around her neck all the time and one day during try-outs, Eva

Perry just strode up to her and asked her what it meant. I mean, none of us even knew the girl. But Alexandra was cool about it.

"I'm Wiccan," she said.

"What?" Eva replied.

"Wiccan. I'm a witch."

I think anywhere else, most people would have been stunned. But not at Hawthorne Day School, the bastion of diversity that it is. Eva simply came back with, "So how many games will that get us?"

"None," Alexandra replied and walked off.

After that, Alexandra, like everyone else, blended into the blur of my school life. So, I was truly surprised when she sat beside me and put the volleyball in my lap.

"I'm very sorry about your father," she said.

I turned to look at her and then through her and then to spit at her feet, but the truth is that I didn't do any of that. She had the most sincere look on her face and all of a sudden, I just wanted to spill my guts. But I managed to hold back the avalanche. I just said, "Thanks."

"I know," she said, "what it feels like to lose a father."

Well, I was stunned. I suppose it was easy for her to read the surprise in my eyes. My world had immediately begun to spin out of control. Alexandra touched my arm as if to stop me; like you would a Lazy Susan. And then I was embarrassed by this sharp breath of air that escaped me on its own, which caused me to slap my hand over my mouth so hard I felt compelled to shout an obscenity. "This is going to sound so silly and so selfish," I said after gathering myself, "but right up until you said that, I guess I must have had the feeling that this had only ever happened to me."

She smiled. "Been there. Done that."

"I'm so sorry. How did he die?" I asked, expecting her to say car crash, cancer, or maybe something a little exotic, befitting a witch. But she had an answer that I certainly wasn't anticipating.

"I don't know if he is dead," she said.

"But you said you lost him."

"I absolutely did."

I'm sure that the look on my face could have been found on dictionary.com right next to the word "confusion."

Alexandra just sadly smiled. "There were bad times," she continued. "Between my mom and dad. I don't really know what happened. I guess I was too young to see it coming. When the screaming and yelling began, it seemed like it happened all of a sudden. Being an only child, I didn't know where to go but to my room and hide under the blankets with my stuffed animals. My teddy bear has been my savior," she said, giving up a soft smile.

"Do you know now what happened?"

"Not really. My mother still won't talk about it, but she stayed and he didn't and I hated him for it. I still do sometimes. Especially since we haven't heard from him."

"Absolutely nothing?"

"Absolutely nothing. But I'm worried. I mean I always worry because I eavesdropped on a conversation between my mother and my Aunt Sarah. She told my aunt that as angry as she was, she was still worried about him. She said she believed he was suicidal and that she was worried that he was in an alley or a ditch or some motel room with a bullet in his head."

Alexandra dropped her head and shook it from side to side.

"I was just turning twelve," she continued, "and I'm listening to my mom say that my dad might have shot himself. I was so worried and I blamed him for making me worry. I hated him for leaving me in this limbo of torture. My mom really went down hill. We limped along for two years until she couldn't deal any more. Finally, my Aunt Sarah showed up, packed us up, and brought us here to live with her. We stayed with her and her family for most of the summer until we found an apartment. We're starting over now. Just like you and your mom."

I found myself struggling to hold back all that I wanted to tell her, to lay out before her. But this time I could not stem the tide. "I know hate," I said.

We just sat there for a minute or two in silence.

"I've really only mentioned it to my grandmother, but sometimes I hate him so much."

"I know that was hard to admit. Especially because I hear that you loved your father very much. That the two of you were really very cool with each other."

I nodded. "He chose someone else over me though and I can't get past that. I just can't. And even worse, he left me to face that fact constantly. To be reminded of it every day I set foot in this building and have to look at her."

"And you hate Heidi too?"

I nodded. "You know her?"

"Well, everybody knows *of* you two."

"She used to be my closest friend. She was the sister I never had and even though she has a little sister, she let me pretend that I was her sister too. Both families were really, really close. When we were in third grade, we made a giant pillow out of squares of fabric during art class. It had a square from each class member and all of our signatures. We put it up to be sold at the school's annual auction. Heidi and I both wanted it badly. It was in the silent auction and my dad stood by it as time ran out to make your bids. Ethan, Heidi's dad, came up just as the waiting period was ending. They both looked at each other knowing that both their girls really, really wanted this pillow. In the end, since my dad was already there, Ethan said, 'It's ok. Heidi won't have it, but at least it stays in the family.' That's how close we all were. Ethan really meant that and my dad never, ever forgot it."

"And it's all changed now?"

"Yes, it's all changed. Hate will do that to a relationship."

"I hear you. I really do."

She took the volleyball from me and held it up in front of us. "Look, Mae. I don't have it all figured out by a long shot. But I feel like I have moved beyond where you are right now. And I just wanted you to know that someone understood your loss and cared that you had to go through it. I just wanted to give you some advice. At least as far as volleyball goes."

"Ok," I said and then I couldn't believe I was accepting advice from anybody at school. Especially from someone that I didn't even know.

"Use it," she said.

"Use what?" I asked, just before it quickly came to me. "The hate?"

"Absolutely. Put a face on this ball. Every time you toss it to be served. Every time it floats in the air above you waiting to be smacked down, put a face on it. Put the face of the person you hate on it. Trust me, it will help you concentrate."

"Did you do this?"

"I did."

"Well, you're a great player. I guess it worked."

Alexandra smiled and put the ball back in my lap and gave me a very long hug that I will always be able to feel. She got up and she walked away. I would like to say that we became best friends after this chat and that she helped me all the way through my struggles, but that wasn't the case. After she left, we never talked about our fathers again. Alexandra never really became good friends with anyone. She came, she graduated, and she disappeared. We were simply a stop on the way to her recovery. There were times though that we passed in the halls, caught each other's eye, smiled, paying silent respect to what we had shared, and quickly moved on.

FOUR

WE STOOD LIKE STRANGERS in an elevator, Mummy and I. Silent, wary, and waiting. But we were not in an elevator. We were at home, in our vestibule, staring through the window of our front door watching the sunlight fade on Hobart Street. We had come to a fork in the road and she had chosen her path. When she looked back for me, I was sitting down, afraid to commit, afraid to go in either direction. And now I was angry with her too because the look in her eyes told me that she must go on without me.

It hurt all the more that she'd chosen to begin this journey with the Fosters. Without Heidi, of course. She was at least sensitive to the fact that had she agreed to Heidi's presence, I would have surely gone over the edge.

They had been calling since the memorial service. Once a week, just to check on us and to suggest that we get together and talk. They wanted to help us heal. Mummy kept begging off until this week, when I heard her say to Grace, Heidi's mom, that she thought it was time. That she thought she could handle it. No, she said, I would not be coming and they could talk about that and would they mind not bringing Heidi, because that would be a deal breaker.

"Mae," she said, "would take that to be something akin to a treasonous act. And I would surely hang for it."

They set the date and time for dining out and then she hung up the phone and turned to me. Mummy knew that she had hurt me and she was assessing the damage.

"I'm sorry, Tragic One," she said just above a whisper.

I refused to let her off the hook so easily. I crossed my arms and showed her my back.

"I just need to begin to move forward," she continued in that same weak and worn-out voice. "I feel as though I have been in a body cast since Daddy died. I just want to break loose and run a bit. That's all, Baby. That's all."

"Oh, Mummy," I thought and I turned to look at that wonderful face. I only wanted the best for her. After all, maybe it had all been so much worse for her. Can the loss of the love of one's life be compared to the loss of a father? Who wins in the I-need-sympathy department? I think I always knew it had to be her.

While I was wallowing and becoming one with my grief, she was dissolving twenty years of a very happy marriage. It may seem harsh to say such a thing, but it was the truth. I mean, technically speaking, she was setting aside a partnership and reassembling a solitary life, except that I would now be tagging along for the ride. She had to go about the business of removing Daddy from her life. First, it was the lawyer and the will. Everything came to her, but now she had to make another will without Daddy's name on it. All of the bills, which had Daddy's name on them because he did the bill paying, had to be changed into her name. The same for bank accounts, insurance, and on and on. One day after school, I came home and decided to listen to Daddy's voice on the answering machine. It was gone, replaced by Mummy's. I cannot imagine how much that whole process had to hurt.

So I uncrossed my arms and gave her a hug.

"I understand," I said, but I felt something shift in how we would remember Daddy from that day forward.

When I saw the Fosters' car drive up and stop in front of the house, I gave Mummy a smile, which she awkwardly returned. I watched as she walked out to meet Grace and Ethan. She hugged them both long and hard. They led her to the car and I watched them pull away. I thought about how I worked so hard to hold Daddy near to me. The closer I kept him to me, the closer I felt to being whole, even during the times that keeping him close left me angry and confused. And so much was confusing. For instance, even though I knew the ongoing and forced clerical separation was extremely hard on her, Mummy seemed to be working hard to push Daddy away. Keeping him close emotionally brought her so much pain. That's why his voice was no longer on the answering machine and that's why she forbade me to look at the old family videos. But now that she had decided to go her own way, I decided that I could, as Gran Gran had said, grieve in my own way.

I went down into the basement playroom, where Daddy and I had spent many days wrestling, doing puzzles, playing card games, sculpting play dough, and painting our faces. He kept the family videos in a cabinet underneath the television and I opened it for the first time since he died. At first, I thought I would start with the rafting trip. The one on which I knew I would see a lot of him. Especially the moment when he got caught joking around and fell out of the raft. Luckily, our guide was a good family friend and she hauled him out of the water and scolded him between fits of uncontrollable laughter.

But in the end, I decided that I wanted to go through our entire life together from the beginning. So, I pulled out the very first tape and loaded it into the VCR, which Daddy'd kept around to play the family videos. There I was rocking in Gran Gran's arms. My first few days of life had been captured in still pictures only because Mummy hadn't wanted a video camera anywhere near her delivery, breast-feeding lessons, or the airy fashions that hospitals tend to favor. So Daddy started videotaping after they brought me home. Mummy was resting in her own bed for the first time since I was born, while Gran Gran took care of me and Daddy put my things away. He'd come back with the camera and there I was, nestled into the arms of his mother. I was in this yellow one-piece thing, with flaps that covered my left hand so I couldn't scratch up my face. I was sucking for dear life on my right thumb and Gran Gran and Daddy laughed. Off to the side and behind Gran

Gran and me was an open box, and peeking out of the top of it was the toddler backpack that I would eventually be carried in for many, many months.

"It's amazing," he said from off camera. "Isn't it?"

Gran Gran looked towards the camera and smiled the gentlest smile.

"I mean me — a father."

"I know," she replied. "I understand how you feel. And I will tell you a secret. As we drove here from the hospital, I was staring at you. I watched you look at Renata and I had the same feeling. It is amazing. My little boy, my only son, my only child, all grown up with a wife and now a baby. You'll never stop looking at Mae that way. Ever."

"I've dreamed of her all my life. Did you know?"

Gran Gran looked surprised. "No, I didn't."

"I dreamed we were in church and I looked down at this little face surrounded by big curly hair and she was saying to me that she wanted to go sit with you and I nodded. She got up and turned and smiled at me as she left the pew, and I watched her skip down the aisle until I saw you reach out and pull her into your lap. The dream has always ended there. It's why I always wanted a girl; why I always knew I would have a girl."

"And here she is."

"Yes, and I am overwhelmed. I can't tell you, Mom, how I feel right now. It just...I don't know. I am just all filled up. I am a very happy man today. Just very happy."

"I know, Sweetie. I know."

Gran Gran couldn't really move but she hugged him with just the look in her eyes. She said "I love you" to him and the camera kind of moved off to one side, up and down and back, and I heard him sigh and give into his tears.

Previously, I'd always mercilessly teased him about the big football player crying over a baby. Maybe I was embarrassed or just subconsciously unable to handle that kind of blatant and tender emotion displayed by the big man in my life. Over the years, I'd listened to this conversation repeatedly because watching the tapes was a favorite pastime of mine, but I just never got it. It's funny how loss changes your perspective. It's only at that moment that I truly heard, understood, and felt the impact my life had upon his.

The next scene was of Mummy's mother, my Grammy, who was leaning over me as I rested in a bouncy seat on the dining room table. She turned away and saw that Daddy had snuck into the room to videotape the moment. Grammy was a little startled and laughed as she backed out of the shot.

"It's ok," Daddy said. "I wanted you in it."

She smiled at him as Mummy was heard calling to her from the kitchen. Before she left, she looked at me and I paused the tape right there and stared at my Grammy until the VCR shut down from being on pause for too long. What all was in that look she gave? I had taken it lightly as well all these years. I had seen all I needed to see for one night. I put the tape back, went upstairs, picked up the phone from Mummy's bedroom, went back to my room, and called Grammy. I didn't tell her about the love I had seen in her eyes. I didn't tell her what it meant to know how happy she was that I was in the world. I just talked about anything and everything and finally told her that I loved her more than I could ever say.

How I wished she had been there with me when Mummy got home from dinner with the Fosters. I was sitting in front of my computer longing to talk to someone. I was lonely. But Gran Gran would have definitely been in bed and I had pushed away everyone else on my buddy list. I couldn't remember a time when my email inbox was empty of anything meaningful to me. I was truly in a bubble. While I was thinking this through and vowing that loneliness would not force me to beg my old friends to allow me back into their good graces, I heard the front door open and shut. The next thing I heard was the well-known (to Daddy and me) thud associated with Mummy's purse hitting the floor and then the not-so-well-known sound of her crying. I couldn't imagine what might have happened during dinner to bring on her tears, but I was thinking, "I told you so."

I ran downstairs to find her standing with her hands on her hips, projecting some very angry body language. As usual, she headed me off at the pass.

"I know, I know," she said. "I just thought it was time. That I was ready to handle it."

"Maybe, just maybe," I replied, "it was never going to be the right time. Maybe even if you waited ten years, it would still hurt."

Mummy smiled and held out her arms and I went to her.

"Thank you, Baby. Thanks."

"No problem."

"I could use a glass of wine."

"Me too."

"Not a chance," she said and slapped me on the butt on her way to the kitchen.

We sat at the table, her with her wine and me with my Pepsi. We talked about how it had seemed easy at first. Hugging Grace and Ethan. Getting in the car. Ethan being his usual hysterical self. It seemed easy until at some point during dinner, when all the forced conversation and humor had run its course, there appeared a lull, and a great big emptiness. A great big hole where there had once been my daddy.

Mummy said the tears started for her and then for Grace and then for Ethan. Then they all laughed a little when it seemed the other diners around them began whispering. But they ignored them, had their cry as an appetizer, and went on to the main course. Grace offered to tell her everything that Heidi had told them about the fire. Mummy agreed but quickly stopped Grace once the story had begun. Ethan told her that Heidi was having a very tough go of it. He told her that the combination of the fire, Daddy's death, and my rejection left her spiraling downward. She was in danger of failing most of her classes and she was not eating properly. They had to put her in therapy. Did Mummy think I would help?

"What did you tell them?" I asked anxiously.

"I told them that you love Heidi."

"I do not!" I shouted.

She ignored my indignation. "I told them that you had your own problems and that frankly, you were in no shape to help anyone. Especially, since you weren't able to help yourself."

She put her face in her hands and her elbows on the table. She stayed like that for some time and the house seemed painfully quiet. Finally, she tilted her head upwards, her red and watery eyes were exposed to me first, just seconds before her quivering lips through which she sort of breathed the words, "Oh, Eddie. What have you done, Baby? What have you done?"

It was the first time I had heard her give voice to what I had been feeling. The first time she let me know that she questioned his actions and was maybe a little angry with him as well. Look at all that had occurred because he decided to run into a burning house. Look at all the lives that had been uprooted and tossed about. Look at all the misery we had to face with only the clichés to comfort us.

"This will only make you stronger."

"You know I truly believe that everything happens for a reason."

"Time heals all wounds."

And on and on. "Why did you do it, Daddy?" I wondered then, as I was prone to do. "Why would you risk everything and leave us like this?"

Mummy continued, "If only you had waited for the firefighters to come. All we would be rebuilding is a house."

She looked at me. "But," she said, "he did what he did and now he's gone. A home is destroyed, two families and relatives all messed up, Heidi is sinking fast carrying the guilt of his death and your anger. And you are being strangled by your anger."

"I cannot believe you are feeling sorry for her! Maybe it's more her fault than Daddy's. If she hadn't freaked out and hid in the closet, there would have been no reason for him to go into the house in the first place. She cost us Daddy!"

"Well, Daddy *is* gone now and she's here and she's dying. The girl can't eat properly; she won't sleep until she's just so exhausted that her body can't go on. She can't talk about it. Her life is ending. This is a lot for her to handle."

Now I was about to blow my top. "Well, what about me, huh? You think it's easy for me?"

"No, I don't. But I don't understand this hatred for someone you loved so much."

"She took from me much more than my love for her."

"I know what you lost," Mummy said. Now she was angry with me, but it came out in more tears and sobs. "I've lost too! I hurt too! At least you can see him and be comforted by what you see. I can't have that. All I can see is his half-burned face and a ravaged body."

"What?" I shouted. "What are you talking about?"

The look on her face told me that she was sorry she had kept something so important from me. She'd felt she was protecting me and though I supposed she was correct, I'm sure it showed on my face that I was not happy about any kind of clandestine act surrounding my daddy's death. I tried to soften my reaction though. Her night had been bad enough. Even I was sensitive enough to understand when it wasn't cool to pile it on.

"The night he died," she said, "after you were asleep and before Grammy and Grandpa arrived, a detective called. He wanted me to come and identify the body. I said I wanted to wait for my parents and it would be in the middle of the night. He said ok and that he would send someone to get us. He said the officer who gave us the news said that it looked as if it was a really good family. A tragedy. Did you get that? He said it *was* a really good family."

I did get it. And I also knew I was getting the real answer as to why Mummy couldn't watch videotapes of Daddy, couldn't keep his picture by her bed, or hear his voice on the answering machine. I moved my chair next to hers and wrapped an arm around her shoulder and laid my head against hers.

"So, anyway," she said. "It was the first thing I said to them when they arrived. They walked in the door and Grammy reached out to hug me, but I stepped back from her and just blurted it out. 'I have to go identify my husband's body.' Grammy hugged me anyway and I called the detective. A police car arrived soon after and took Grandpa and me to the morgue. Grammy wanted to stay with you. She thought you'd wake up and need to have someone here. So we get to the morgue and it was just like on television. A guy in a white coat meets us with his clipboard. He guides Grandpa, me, and the officer into a big room. There is one wall full of what looks like big file cabinets, but I know that they don't contain any paperwork. It really begins to hit me that I am surrounded by death and that this man in front of me is some kind of Dr. Frankenstein. We follow the good doctor past a row of tables to one table underneath a big light. Unceremoniously, he unzips the heavy black bag on the table and the next thing I know, I'm sitting on the floor. I guess I sort of fainted and I began to laugh at finding myself on the seat of my pants. But I quickly remembered what put me there. I quickly remembered that I had just seen your daddy. Half of his face was burned away. All that I could see of his body was burned. But the unburned half of his face was enough. I'd know that face or any part of it anywhere. Right there, at that place, I thought about mornings when I would wake up and he was still asleep. I thought about me just staring at that face and thinking, 'I'm married to this good and gentle man. What will our lives be like? Will I still be this happy with him when we are old?' Well, we know that's not an issue any more."

I squeezed tighter.

"Every time I think of him, I see that half-face before I see anything else. And it just about kills me. I find myself just trying to put him out of my mind. I just can't take seeing that face. It tells me that he must have been in so much pain."

I just kept holding on.

Mummy just kept talking. When she was done, her wine glass was empty, her hair mussed from all the times she pulled it or ran her hands through it, her eyes red and tired, and her mouth trembled. Oh, Mummy, my Mummy. How could we have been in the same house, suffering all that we had suffered and not have shared this until now?

I took my mother upstairs. I undressed her as if she were my child, put her in her big sleeping t-shirt, and set another glass of wine on her bedside table. I really didn't care if she needed to get drunk. That night I listened and learned. That night I decided that I would never harp on her again about watching the family videos or turning down photos, including the one next to the glass of wine I'd just set down. I opened the drawer of her bedside table and put the picture inside, on top of the business card from the nice officer whose news had rocked our world.

I got myself ready for bed and joined Mummy. By the time I was under the covers, she was asleep, the wine untouched. Her face was tight and her eyes darted here and there beneath her eyelids. Her breathing was loud and strained. I wondered, was she looking at Daddy? I knew then that I was lucky. My vision of him, whenever I could hold on to it, would always be of a lively, happy face. Every memory for her would include that flash. That fleeting moment of pain.

I reached across her and turned out the light. I lay back waiting for sleep, fearing the dream that I knew would come. Staring into the darkness, I wondered, is this how we will forever remember him? Not as the man we loved, but as the man who destroyed so many lives while trying to save just one.

FIVE

THE NEXT AFTERNOON, I stood at the end line waiting to practice my serve. The coach stood with her arms folded across her chest, impatiently waiting for me to perform the usual, shall I say, creative serve. This, she knew, was to be followed by my customary self-loathing and the quickstep to a seat in the bleachers, freeing her to go on with practice without distraction.

I dropped the ball.

Literally, I mean. My hands were a little shaky that day and I just lost control of it. The coach then let fly with a sigh that might have registered on the Richter scale. I quickly considered just going to the bleachers without trying, but the ball came back to me before I had the chance to move. It came back by way of Alexandra Carr, who rolled it to me and said quickly and quietly with soft eyes and a gentle smile, "Use it." She had been giving me that look for some time now. Since our conversation, I'd had trouble with the idea of putting a face on the ball, leaving me entrenched in the same rut that I had been in all season long. But this day was different. I wanted to try and after spending the night next to a tortured mother, there was no doubt whose face would appear first on the volleyball. I cupped it in my left hand at eye level and all of a sudden I could not fight the appearance of Daddy on the ball. I thought of Alexandra's smile and it gave me the strength to accept the face on the ball and what I would do to it.

I rocked in my stance and tossed up the ball. Fueled by anger, my swing was strong, hard, and focused. The serve was my serve, the same one that in the past had won many games for my team. They all stared except Alexandra Carr, who understood. The coach came out of her trance and shouted, "Where the hell did that come from?" Volleyball had become volleyball again.

The rest of that practice, I ran, jumped, slid, dove, and otherwise chased my father on the ball. My coaches and teammates were stunned by the sudden transformation. When practice was over and with my father's image slowly fading on the ball, I sat alone again on the bleachers too exhausted to cry even though I wanted to. It had been a physically and emotionally demanding practice and I needed to sit for a while before I could even walk to the locker room.

For the next week I practiced like my life depended on a successful session. And although the coach didn't want to play me because it wouldn't be fair to the girls who had worked hard all season, she was still the coach who had been happy to sit me down because she wanted to win. So eventually, she sat down another girl and I started.

There were only a few games left in the regular season but I started them. Alexandra and I dominated play and we won them all going away. Gran Gran and Pop Pop even came to see me play in our first game of the league tournament. We went all the way to the finals where we lost, but we felt good about ourselves and we would have our revenge the following season. By then I wouldn't need Daddy or Heidi Foster on the ball.

It was now nearing Thanksgiving and I had reconquered volleyball, maintained straight As, and begun to find some peace within my bubble. I was still the "Tragic One" and I still carried my anger for all the traitors at school, but I would be lying if I didn't say that I was finding a comfort zone even if it rested on the fault line called Heidi Foster. She and I had both become like ghosts in the hallways and classrooms. People looked at us as if they'd seen something strange and unsettling, then moved on with the hairs on the back of their necks standing straight up. Heidi was even spookier than me. She seemed to be there one moment and then gone the next. Of course, what was really happening was that she was starting to miss more and more school. When she was there, she was in a trance broken only by the startled look on her face when she found herself face to face with my anger as we passed in the hallways or when we were forced to feel each other's presence from across a classroom. I was much happier on the days that she stayed home, and I began to pray for them every morning as I walked up the stairs to the school.

Other people were praying also. Just not for the same outcome as me. My old friends Ellie and Charlotte made this plain when they cornered me in a bathroom one afternoon. Technically speaking, they kidnapped me. I mean, it was my understanding that any time someone took away your right to move freely and restricted your comings and goings, you were being kidnapped. I explained this to them as they closed the door and blocked my access to it.

"Oh, screw you, Mae," was Charlotte's ruling on the issue.

"Why, Charlotte," I replied, my hand across my chest, feigning the surprise of the most innocent of southern belles. But truthfully, I was quite stunned by the whole situation and I am sure it showed on my face. They had me and they knew it. There was no time for me to get the anger positioned correctly on my face. No time to prepare my eyes to stare right through them. No time to make them so uncomfortable that they would want to leave me alone. Ellie stood right in front of me, so angry that she was shivering.

"You!" she shouted, pointing her finger in my face. "You need to get it together. I can't believe you. Heidi could have died. She's still in shock and she's wasting away. I know what you feel, but she's still alive. You need to help her or we will have lost two lives."

This knocked my sense of anger right back in place. I could not believe what I was hearing.

"She could have died?" I questioned. "My father DID die! Got that? DID DIE!"

"We know that," Charlotte replied. "And we understand that and we have tried to console you but you weren't having any of it."

"Because you were spending all of your time consoling her. You made your choice."

"No," Charlotte shot back, "You made the choice to shut everybody out."

"And I am glad I did because you guys just don't get it."

"We just said that we know what you're feeling," Ellie said. "Charlotte just told you that we are aware, just in case you didn't think we were, that your father died."

"You know what I am feeling?" I asked, my eyes filling with even more anger and new tears. I dropped the hammer. "You don't know Jack."

Now it was my turn to do the pointing. "Do you say goodnight to your father before you go to bed?"

"Yes," Ellie replied.

"Do you?" I pointed at Charlotte.

"Yes."

"Then that must mean your fathers are alive. Which would mean you have no way — and I mean absolutely no way — of knowing what the hell I feel! You can still kiss your father in the morning, hug him when you feel like it, take walks with him and you can still say 'I love you' to a live human being who will grab you and hold you and say 'I love you too' and will tell you that you are the best daughter in the whole wide world. You still have all of this and it was taken away from me. I hurt. I hurt like hell. I hurt so much I felt like dying and I feel like dying every time I think of my daddy burning alive. And, by the way, I think of that every single day. Now," I said looking from one to the other. "You want to tell me again that you really know how I feel?"

Now it was their turn to be stunned.

"No," Charlotte said. "No, I don't think we do."

"No, I didn't think you did," I replied grinding in the guilt like a discarded cigarette butt on a sidewalk. "And don't ever say to me that *we* might be losing two lives. You haven't lost a thing and if all you care about is Heidi, then you don't really care that I have lost anything. You both have siblings. I am the only child of two only children. I can't afford to keep losing people."

I took a step toward Charlotte and Ellie, and they parted so that I could walk unobstructed out the door and into the security of my anger, which I managed to display proudly until the Thanksgiving holiday arrived.

SIX

I LEFT SCHOOL EARLY on the Wednesday before Thanksgiving. Most of the school was gathered in the student forum for a holiday assembly. I was so ready for the holiday break that I couldn't wait to leave, so I quietly gathered my belongings and slipped out of a side door. As I began my walk home, I felt free. After my fight with Ellie and Charlotte, word got around that I was an absolute loss and that I truly didn't care what happened to Heidi. All the anger I had been dishing out began to come back to me. Now I was actively being ostracized. It was hard not to feel the pressure but I refused to break. At this point, I believed that I had already lost them all anyway.

So as I hit the pavement, I thought happily about four days of peace. Four days to not see anyone. Four days to lie in bed. Four days to stare at Frodo Baggins, listen to music, and to find some comfort in the quiet of my room. But then I suddenly became fearful of the quiet. Something always seemed to creep into my silence and ruin the day. As I walked, it occurred to me that this would be my first holiday without my father. I still had not reached the point where most of my joyful moments were untouched by the memory of his death.

I walked into my house and tossed my backpack into the mudroom, promising myself not to think of any homework until the next morning. I started having visions of Mummy and me eating popcorn and chewing on Milk Duds at the movies. But just as my backpack hit the floor, I heard footsteps and out of the kitchen walked my Grammy. I was surprised and I was so happy to see her. She held on to me for quite some time and I allowed her to just swallow me up.

"I don't have to ask how you are," she said, holding me now at arms length. "I see a young girl who is unmistakably emotionally whipped."

I smiled and looked into that wonderful face and I wondered what it was about me that was so easily read by both my grandmothers. I wondered how they could just look at me and know everything. I would have the same feeling later on when I finally made it to my bedroom to see that I had email. It was from Gran Gran.

Her email read:

> "Hi, Mae. I have been thinking about you all morning. I was thinking that this will be your first holiday without your dad. Pop Pop and I feel it too. I know that your Grammy and Grandpa will be there for you, but if you need to hear our voices please feel free to call. Otherwise, we will talk to

you tomorrow before you sit down for dinner. I love you truly."

But at that moment, I just wanted to study Grammy and have her study me. I wanted her to tell me that I would make it through this long and painful journey. We played my favorite game, a pattern-finding game called SET. We listened to music and talked about school. We took a walk and I told her neighborhood stories about each house. When Mummy got home with Grandpa, who had gone to spend the afternoon with her at her office, Grammy and I had already planned the night. We went out to dinner and to an action movie that I am sure no one liked but me. It was the kind of thing that Daddy and I went to see together, so they endured it and were surprisingly supportive.

That night I lay in bed next to Mummy. I told her how happy I was that Grammy and Grandpa had surprised me for Thanksgiving. Mummy smiled and brushed my hair with her hand.

"I thought it would be special for you," she said. "I just didn't feel like driving to Boston or Smithfield this year."

"Speaking of Smithfield, I got an email from Gran Gran. She knew about Grammy and Grandpa."

"Are you surprised?"

"A little. But I guess that's kind of stupid. I mean I can't believe that I thought you would never speak to them again since Daddy was no longer in our lives. He was your only bridge to them though."

"That's true and maybe a lot of in-laws do fade away, but I really love Daddy's parents. Also," she continued, "We have a new bridge now. You."

"I guess that's right."

"They will always want to be in your life and I will do whatever is necessary to make that happen. Truth be told, I talk to Gran Gran almost every other day."

"Wow," I said. "That makes me feel comforted. Thank you for not letting go."

She reached out and pulled me to her and I spent the night there. When I woke up sweating from my dream, she held me until I went back to sleep. But later in the night, I woke up again. This time I hadn't dreamed about my father. This time I dreamed about two little girls on a school playground. They had tears in their eyes and their faces were stricken with anger. They stood next to the tire swing near the big wooden and plastic play station called the Big Toy. They were screaming bloody murder.

SEVEN

I WOKE UP ON THANKSGIVING MORNING caught in the bear hug of a late autumn breeze. It felt soooo good. I moaned and pulled my blanket and sheets tighter around me, burrowing deeper into the morning peace. Mummy was up and gone, but she'd cracked the bedroom windows before she left. Now, I slowly opened my eyes and watched the curtains billowing out into the room, pushed by the cool November air. I heard faint laughter in the distance and it took me a while to realize that it was coming from inside rather than outside of the house. I was surprised. It had been a long time since I had heard such a commotion in our home. It softened me.

I knew what was probably happening. Grandpa loved to read and I knew that he was doing just that on the couch under the big south-facing windows in the family room. I also knew that Grammy and Mummy were doing their usual telling of old stories, which made fun at his expense. I saw them standing in the kitchen, which opens into the family room, just having a good old time. While protesting on the outside, I knew that he truly loved the attention. I used to sit at his feet when I was little, and when the abuse was at its peak, he would look hurt when they turned to him, but he would wink and smile at me when they looked the other way. All of this just made me close my eyes and smile.

The next thing I knew, I was being shaken awake by Mummy. She was holding the phone from the kitchen in her hand. I stole a quick glance at the one next to the bed because I didn't hear it ring and she smiled. "I turned the ringer off," she said.

"You're too good to me," I said.

"Well, it's about time you recognized that fact."

I sat up and smiled.

"It's Gran Gran," she said.

I took the phone and she left the room.

"Happy Thanksgiving, Gran Gran. How are you guys doing?"

"Happy Thanksgiving to you too, Sweetie. We're both doing well. It feels a little lonely today. Not that you all came here for every Thanksgiving anyway, but it is different when you can't even call. When you can't even hear his voice."

"I know," I said. "I feel you."

"But Pop Pop and I have been trying to stay positive. We have been laughing some too. We've been talking about how your dad always said that Christmas was his favorite holiday, but we really think it was Thanksgiving."

"Really. Why do you say that?"

"Sweetie, for a man like your daddy, Thanksgiving must have been heaven on earth. Think about it. All of the women he loves fussing over all of his favorite foods. Football all day long with Pop Pop or your Grandpa and then more food. You know your dad."

I had to laugh. "True! So true, Gran Gran. I never thought of it quite that way before. I bet Mummy will get a kick out of that theory."

We both shared a laugh and some love. I spoke briefly to Pop Pop, who told me that they were going to a cousin's for dinner and that they would check in again before bedtime. I told him that I looked forward to that.

"How 'bout them Cowboys!" we shouted at each other over the phone.

We hung up, the both of us thinking of Daddy and his favorite football team.

The warm shower felt good that morning and I stayed in it for a long time. Normally, Mummy would yell into the bathroom, "The water company just called. The city water supply just dried up. Would you know anything about that?" But today, she never came and I began to reflect on the third dream I had, the one that came to me earlier that morning. I dreamed about the two girls again. About how truly upset they were with each other and how the teachers could not console either of them. The girls were Heidi and me.

We were not in the same first grade class and we only saw each other during recess or assemblies. I do know that we didn't like each other, but I cannot remember why. It was like we just looked at each other the wrong way when we first met. After that, we seemed to be at war over everything. If she was in the sandbox, that is where I wanted to be and I let her know that she had taken my place. If I were on the zip line, she would grab me and stop me mid-zip and leave me hanging in mid-air. The morning when the teachers finally had enough of us, I don't remember what we were fighting about. That was the funny thing. When they took us to the principal's office, we were crying uncontrollably. She sat us down and asked, "Ok, why don't you tell me what this is all about?" Neither of us could tell her. She called our parents and looking back, it was lucky for us that they could only reach the fathers.

We stood outside of the school between them, still trying to stop crying. Our dads shook hands and apologized for each other's daughter and we turned to walk away, to go home, and participate in a lecture about appropriate behavior and how we would look forward to a better tomorrow. But Ethan had a better idea.

"Hey, guys," he called to us. "I know this little place call Jetties. Just a block away. You know the one?"

Daddy nodded.

"What do you say we not go home angry? I think this kind of situation just screams for some ice cream."

Daddy smiled and nodded. Then, off we went.

We stayed for more than an hour as Ethan kept us laughing and laughing and laughing. He was definitely at his best that day. I still remember getting in the car and forgetting about everything except how good that ice cream tasted and how Heidi and I giggled and leaned on each other over and over again as Ethan made us laugh. That was the beginning of everything between Heidi and me.

As I got out of the shower, as much as I didn't want to, I smiled. And I was touched by that memory and all the memories after that until the day my daddy died.

I put her out of my mind.

Downstairs I found the three of them still laughing. Mummy had tears in her eyes. They were telling tales about her high school days back in Boston. I sat beside Grandpa, who leaned over and kissed me on the cheek. I just listened for a while and from time to time Mummy seemed embarrassed for me to be hearing some of the stories. And I must admit that I did file many of them away for further use. Or should I say abuse. However, as time wore on, I began to recognize that they seemed stuck in the past. I almost felt like an intruder because they seemed to be reaching back for a comfortable place before Daddy and me, when it was just the three of them. I felt happy knowing though that this was how Mummy had been raised. Happy, comfortable, and loved. Just as I had been before Daddy died. Still, I wanted one of them to acknowledge him. Eventually, it happened although not as I would have wanted it to.

We were sitting at the dinner table. The blessing had been said without mentioning Daddy. Just a thank you God for everything good that has ever happened, now let's eat. After we were fat and happy and just hanging around the table, Grandpa brought down the thunder.

"By the way, you were going to tell me who that fellow was at your office. You know the one who we kept accidentally bumping into all afternoon?" he said with a wry smile.

"Oh, Daddy," Mummy said. "He's just a coworker. We've worked together for twelve years."

"Your father is pretty good at these things, my dear," Grammy said. "No need to play coy."

"Oh, what the hell. He's been putting the moves on me for a couple of weeks now. But I told him that I wasn't anywhere near ready for anything like that."

"Well, if he's following you around all day, I guess he's ready."

They laughed.

"You are a beautiful woman," Grandpa said leading Mummy towards something.

"And you are going to be attracting a lot of attention," Grammy added.

Mummy said, "I suppose that's a good thing."

"Why of course it is," Grammy continued.

It was about this time that they noticed I was not participating in the conversation any longer. It was about this time that they recognized that my eyes were red and my face was streaked with tears.

"Oh, Mae," Grammy said, picking up on the reason for my distress right away. "It's only natural. It's just the way of things."

I looked at Mummy, hoping for a contradiction to Grammy's philosophy of love and relationships. Mummy did not speak, yet she got her point across just the same. I can be truthful and tell you that up until this moment, I hadn't given this much thought at all. But the wave washed over me quickly and left me dripping with a moment of truth and a kind of sadness. I looked in her face and without speaking, she'd let me know that she had no intention of spending the rest of her life alone.

Grandpa reached out, grabbed my hands, and turned me to him. "Do you think your dad would want her to live alone from now on?"

Well, I knew my dad and I know that he would have agreed with Grandpa. But I didn't hear him say it, so it was all speculation. I mean, if he had died of cancer and on his death bed made Mummy promise not to live the rest of her life pining away for him, it would be easy for me. But he didn't die that way and I didn't hear him say it, so it was hard to come to grips with.

"No, he wouldn't have wanted that," I finally said.

Grandpa patted my hands and Grammy reached over to run her hands gently through my hair.

I asked softly, "Then who will remember him?"

They all looked shocked by this question, so I accepted the responsibility of making my point absolutely crystal clear.

"Mummy always said that to have a good marriage, two people had to trust each other and not be afraid to be vulnerable. They had to do this in order to give everything they had emotionally and physically to their partner, to make sure that they had a solid marriage."

"I did say that on occasion," Mummy replied.

"So if that is true, then you will have to put Daddy out of your life and heart to give everything to another man. Right? All the special things he gave you have to go to the attic or be given away. The pictures of the two of you have to be boxed up. You'll have to almost erase him to satisfy another man's love and attention. Right?"

Complete silence.

"Well, am I right?" I asked a little louder than I should have.

Still silence. No one argued with me at all. So, I took that as a yes.

"So who will remember him besides me?"

"We all will remember him, Baby," Mummy said. "Especially me. I spent twenty years with your father and I loved him with all my heart. I won't — or better yet — I can't ever forget him."

"But you are already primed to put him aside. You all agree that you will do it and by not telling this guy at work that you will never be ready, you have put yourself on the road to being ready. I don't want my daddy to fade. I don't want to lose him. You may get married again, but don't ever expect me to think of your husband as my father or even stepfather. The word 'father' used in relationship to me in any way, shape, or form will always mean my daddy and no other man."

Mummy nodded. She had that very serious look that I knew so well. The one that said she'd seen the light.

"I hear you, Baby," she said. "I understand."

"And," I continued, "I never want to live in this house with you married to another man."

"Now, Mae," Grammy started, but was quickly cut off by a swipe of Mummy's hand.

"I hear you, Baby," Mummy said again. "I do."

I got up and left the table. I went down to the basement to watch video tapes and I didn't care who said I shouldn't. And I was prepared to offer some physical resistance to anyone who came down to stop me. But no one did.

In this particular video, I was just under a year old, toddling and crawling around our backyard. My friend Jordan Richards is there and eventually we end up sitting in the sandbox throwing sand at each other while our fathers talk. I didn't want to lose Daddy, although I knew that without the videotape, he would have already been fading.

By the time the Cowboys had won their game and had set off to have a late dinner with their families, I was calling Gran Gran and explaining to her that I wanted everything of Daddy's that I could find. Everything that she and Pop Pop could stand to part with. I wanted to collect all the stories anyone ever told about him and I would put this all together to have and hold on to forever and forever.

EIGHT

ON THE MONDAY AFTER THANKSGIVING, I had a revelation. I stood in the entrance hall of school recognizing that my four days away had been more than just your regular holiday adjournment. I quickly realized that I had been on a four-day anger fast. I knew this because I was staring straight at Heidi Foster and instead of feeling my blood boil, I found myself thinking of the two of us and the British girl band, The Spice Girls. I reached deep inside for the anger that I always kept in stock, but my system seemed to have been flushed almost clean. I struggled to hold on to what I could find. Maybe it was just four straight days away from the struggle. Maybe it was Grammy and Grandpa being around. Maybe it was sleeping late on Thanksgiving morning. Maybe it was the memories that kept creeping into my mind. Who really knows? I only knew that I was operating at a serious hate deficit.

Heidi was at the other end of the hall, walking towards me. There seemed to be several things different about her.

She was walking at a normal pace. Before the holiday, she was struggling for every step and always had her eyes to the floor. But she was looking straight ahead at me and while she was still very, very pale, she seemed much calmer. But the thing that struck me most was that she was alone. Up until now, she always had one of her friends (my old friends) with her. The school administration didn't want her to be alone. I guess they cared, but I think they surely didn't want a suicide committed on their watch. Not good for fundraising and the like.

So I decided that the people who couldn't stand to be around me any more couldn't stand to be around her either. Maybe they'd had just about enough of our drama. Maybe it was just the two of us again, even though I had no intention of moving past the warm memory in my mind.

We were in second grade and by then we were a serious part of each other's lives. We were at each other's side all day long at school. There were often short play dates after school and longer play dates and sleepovers on the weekends. Daddy always smiled when he opened the door for Heidi when she arrived at our house. He was so happy because she felt right at home. She'd rush past him yelling a quick "hello" and off she'd run to my room. Sometimes, she'd even run into the kitchen, grab a glass on the way to the fridge for some milk, and then be in our play room before my parents knew she was in the house. I felt equally comfortable at Heidi's house. I remember walking into their family room to begin to ask for something to drink only to have Grace just wave her hand at me and tell me to help myself. "You know where everything is," she'd said. It was my second home.

One day, while playing at Heidi's, we began discussing things all the rage, the most important of which on that particular day was The Spice Girls. They championed "girl power," in which Heidi and I were big believers. We sang their hit "Wannabe" over and over again. In the halls, on the playgrounds, all over the place. "So tell me what you want, what you really, really want," we sang, on and on and on. Then at the peak of our Spice Girl worship, Daddy set up his video camera and hooked it up to our television. He had spot lights and a disco ball that hung from the ceiling, spinning tiny, bright reflections all over the room. Heidi and I dressed up for the part and we sang almost that entire album while watching ourselves on the television as Daddy videotaped our playroom gala. It was just one night, but it was a big night. It's funny, you know. The times that seem so trivial end up meaning so much.

But as I came closer to meeting Heidi in the hallway, I refused to let this fleeting diversion into niceness break me. So, I reached down deep inside to try to regain my storm of ill humor. The trouble was that my unintentional anger fast had been a little too successful. So I struggled and as I got closer to her, I became anxious about the fact that she might see through me and it left me a little discombobulated. However, my distress turned out to be good enough. I am sure she recognized and internalized her effect upon me as the gap between us rapidly closed. I know this because her stride went off a little and she stumbled. Her face tightened. As I passed by her, I could see that while she may have moved a little more toward being her old self, she still had a long way to go. Her face was still quite pale and her eyes were watery and, better yet, very, very needy. As I left her to whatever errand she was on, I knew she was still hurting and that made me happy.

NINE

Gran Gran: How are you, Sweetie?

The Tragic One: Good…good.

Gran Gran: Well, that's a step in the right direction.

The Tragic One: Maybe. Jury's still out.

Gran Gran: What have you been up to?

The Tragic One: The usual. To school. To home. To homework.

Gran Gran: Well, it's almost time for another break from all of that. Are you happy? Or are you afraid you'll be cleansed of more anger?

The Tragic One: Yes to both. But I need to remain hostile. Otherwise, she will feel she got away with it.

Gran Gran: Well, I'm pleased with part of that answer. I didn't know if you would be happy.

I think Christmas will be very hard for your mom. You know how much she gets into the holiday season. When your dad was new to dating her, he once wrote to me that being with your mom around Christmas time was like being a child again. She gets that excited and it's catching, he told me. He just loved it!

The Tragic One: I know. I'm not really looking forward to it.

Gran Gran: Are you guys sure you want to spend it alone? You could come here or go to Boston.

The Tragic One: No, Mummy is firm on this one. She wants to celebrate together. She says we have to start to handle life as we are, you know. The two of us now.

Gran Gran: I understand. I really do. Maybe I just want you here to help me make it through.

The Tragic One: I'm sorry, Gran Gran.

Gran Gran: Oh, it's all right, Sweetie. Your mom is right. We all have to reconfigure and move ahead. The best way to do that is to face the loss head-on. In truth, no Christmas will ever be the same.

The Tragic One: Unfortunately true.

Gran Gran: But since Christmas won't go away, what do you want us to put under your tree?

The Tragic One: Oh, I really don't want anything. I'm going to use the time to work on my project.

Gran Gran: How's that going?

The Tragic One: Pretty good. Mummy opened up their photo box for me. She gave me his scrapbook from college. You know, all the football stuff and friend stuff too. Some personal cards and letters. She said she wants to keep the letters he wrote to her. If she ever remarries, I will get them. Otherwise, I have to wait until — ...well, you know.

Gran Gran: That seems fair.

The Tragic One: It does. I'm happy with that. All I want to do is put together a record of the man I loved and still love. Something tangible, something physical that I can hold on to and remember. I have to be caretaker of his memory. I have to keep him with us. You know what I mean?

Gran Gran: Oh, I know. You're preaching to the choir. It's one of my goals every day I wake up. Every day.

The Tragic One. Well, I gotta go now. Mummy's calling for dinner. I love you, Gran, Gran.

Gran Gran: I love you too, Sweetie. I truly do!

Another videotape. Christmas-time and I was three years old. We, the three of us, were on a mission to visit

Santa Claus at the Georgetown Park Mall. It was a mission of some significance. At this point, I was convinced that if I didn't see Santa, there would be no Christmas, which meant no toys either. This fact presented a problem for Mummy and Daddy when we found Santa's big red chair, but no Santa. I was quite upset, which is painfully obvious on the videotape that Daddy had been recording on since we'd turned the corner to Santa's house. He kept it running as he and Mummy, half laughing at my craziness and half taking me seriously, tried to calm me down. But in the midst of all my drama, the world was quickly calmed when who should appear but the jolly old man himself, fresh from his break. He recognized right away the affliction that had befallen me.

"Where you looking for me?" he asked.

"Yes," I replied, hiccoughing through my tears.

"Well," he said, "I had to take a little break. You see Rudolph and the rest of the reindeer are in a special tent on the roof. I needed to check on them."

All tears halted at the notion of actual reindeer on the roof of my mall in the middle of Washington, DC. On camera, I am suddenly wide-eyed and at full attention.

Right there, in the middle of the mall aisle, Santa asked me what I wanted and I rattled off my list. He kept nodding at me and winking over my shoulder at Mummy and Daddy. Finally, when I was done listing things, I told him that there would be milk and cookies waiting.

"Yum, yum," he said while rubbing his hands together. "But don't forget my reindeer. They work very hard and they get hungry too."

"What do they eat?" I asked.

"Rice Krispies."

"Rice Krispies?"

"Yes, Rice Krispies. Do you have some at home?"

"Do we, Mummy?" I asked, my face beginning to show a little despair. I imagined that I was just a bit worried that if we didn't have some Rice Krispies, Santa might not stop at my house. But, as usual, Mummy had my back.

"Luckily," she answered. "It's one of Daddy's favorites."

A huge smile appeared on my face and Santa shook my hand. I didn't get a picture with him, but I doubt that any of the kids who were busy lining up at his big red chair got the special attention I did that day.

But that was then. Now, years later, it was just the two of us at Georgetown Park Mall. We wandered the aisles staring at the decorations, people watching, and being overwhelmed by Christmas music. Mummy had thought a trip to the mall would help get us in the mood for the holidays, but the longer we walked, the more we realized that it was a lost cause. We were just marching through tradition that was no longer tradition. We didn't even buy anything. All we did was manage to get depressed, so we decided to leave. But on the way out, we saw Santa sitting in his big red chair and there was not much of a line. We looked at each other and Mummy said, "What the hell?"

So we found ourselves, a grown woman and a fourteen-year-old girl, each sitting on one of Santa's knees. When he asked us what we wanted for Christmas, we weren't exactly Johnny-on-the-spot ready with an answer. We just stared at each other until Mummy finally spoke.

"Just each other," she said, softly. "Just each other."

"Wish granted!" Santa bellowed. "You girls are easy."

With that, we had our picture taken and we were out the door.

On Christmas Eve, we went to the movies and bypassed all of our normal traditions. No singing of carols, no reading the manger story from the Bible, no reading of *A Christmas Carol*, no milk and cookies, and no Rice Krispies for Rudolph and the boys.

"Let's start new traditions next year," I offered.

Mummy agreed.

Christmas morning there were gifts under the tree. Mummy got a portable DVD player from Grandpa. It was for business trips. Mummy always complained about her inability to sleep on airplanes, a problem that was exacerbated by the terrible on-board movie selection.

"This oughta do just fine," she said.

Grammy gave her an absolutely beautiful business suit to wear on some of those trips. I really, really liked it.

"Can I like borrow that from time to time?" I asked.

"When you, like, get a job," she replied.

I burst out laughing. Mummy could be so crazy sometimes.

Grandpa and Grammy gave me an iTunes account so that I could download music anytime I wanted. I promised Mummy that I would not overdo it. It was a great gift that continued until I graduated from college.

From Gran Gran and Pop Pop, Mummy received some recent fiction releases and a really comfy lay-around-the-house sweater that I did, like, actually borrow. For me, there was a very large box left under the tree. I opened it and simply put, it floored us. For the next four or five hours we just sat on the floor by the tree, patiently going through my father's life. There was his birth certificate from Louise Obici Memorial hospital just outside of Suffolk, Virginia. It was complete with his thumb prints and those from his precious little feet. There were letters and cards from friends and family of Gran Gran and Pop Pop, wishing them and their new baby well. A picture of my paternal great-grandparents making their first visit. Pictures of his first Christmas and baptismal. Pictures of him speaking at kindergarten graduation. His report cards, which indicated that Daddy was a very good student, but that he talked too much. Mummy and I laughed at that one. "Tell us something we don't know," we said, laughing.

So we went on like this, through camp participation awards, ribbons for Presidential fitness, karate, football, prom, English and history papers, and science fair projects. And the most special item of all was his high school Letterman's jacket. It was blue and gold, with letters on either side of the front recognizing his efforts on the football field. I put it on immediately and I wore it constantly. Every time I put it on, it felt like a hug.

TEN

WHILE IT WAS TRUE that no Christmas would ever be the same again, I decided that this holiday had indeed been successful. After all, we did have Daddy with us. Because of Gran Gran, who really paid attention during our last instant messaging session, Mummy and I discovered a whole new Eddie. Mummy knew many of the stories, and she'd actually seen some of the items like the report cards. But there were many discoveries for her and of course, everything was new to me. A treasure chest of memories, laughter, and love. When we finally called Gran Gran to thank her, she had been sitting around wondering if she'd made a mistake or not. We assured her that she was absolutely golden.

I was happy, which was something special in and of itself, and Christmas morning set me up perfectly to emotionally carry out my own plan of discovery.

A couple of weeks before, I'd gone into Mummy's room. I opened the drawer of her bedside table and there was the photo of Daddy, face down. I picked it up and looked at it. He stood on a cliff in Mendocino, California. He was looking toward Mummy, who was taking the photo. A smile on his face, the Pacific at his back.

I kissed the photo and placed it back exactly as it had been, except for the business card that had been hidden beneath it. It was the card given to Mummy by the police officer who had delivered the bad news those few months ago.

I dialed the number on the card and his precinct answering service picked up the call. When a person came on line, I asked for Officer Cooper Bradley. They told me that he was on patrol, but that they would get the message to him, so I sat at home and waited. I remember downloading a few songs, making lunch, and sitting down to watch another videotape. An hour or so later, the call came. Officer Bradley said he'd been expecting, or rather, hoping to hear from our house, but that he'd thought the phone call would have come from Mummy.

"Why did you expect a call?" I asked.

"Well," he replied, "people usually want to know more than you two did when the news of a death is given. I thought you might need to know more eventually. You know, finish the story."

I smiled to myself because that's exactly what I was hoping to do. He truly had my number.

"And," he continued, "in truth I left your house feeling very attached to your particular situation. I've wanted to help, but I didn't want to bother you. But now, I'm happy to be talking to you. How can I be of assistance?"

"I am searching for all of my father's life," I replied. "From the beginning to the end. I have the beginning pretty much taken care of. I wondered if you might help me with the end."

"I will do my very best. Let me guess. You want the police report?"

"I do. Is it a matter of public record, like they say on the cop shows? I was thinking it would be very helpful to me."

"Yes, it is. But I was thinking that we could do better."

"How so?" I asked, feeling a wave of excitement rush over me.

"Let me make some phone calls and let's talk after Christmas. I have some time between then and New Year's. We'll get together then."

"Ok," I said. "Thank you so much."

"Believe me, Mae," he replied, "the pleasure is all mine."

After Christmas, I told Mummy what I had done. She wasn't very happy with me. Officer Bradley had given me his home number before hanging up and Mummy decided that she would give him a call. When he came to the phone, she just flew past the small talk and blurted out, "Why are you doing this?"

"Isn't it obvious?" I was thinking as she listened to his answer. While he spoke, her face softened and she turned to look at me with big doey, caring eyes.

"Ok," she said. "That's enough reason for me. I get it." She hung up the phone. "Let's go shopping."

"For what?"

"One of those fancy, new miniature tape recorders. That wonderful man has set up interviews with people who were there that day. Witnesses, the firemen, and himself of course. You can't commit all of this to memory."

The next day Mummy went to work and I took the metro to Officer Bradley's house. His very pretty and very pregnant wife opened the door.

"Hello, Mae," she said, smiling. "We're so glad that you are here. Come on in."

She led me through the more formal part of the house into their family room. There were boxes everywhere. She apologized, saying that presents for the baby were already arriving. It made her nervous to get them before the birth, but she could hardly be upset with their family and friends who were so excited about the latest addition-to-be.

"Do you know what you're having?" I asked.

A big smile grew quickly across her face. "We do. It's a little girl. And she'll be named Doris after her father's mother. A little old fashioned, I know, but we really like that name."

"I do too, actually," I replied, putting two and two together and coming up with the reason Mummy went soft on the phone with Officer Bradley.

By the time we were seated at the kitchen table having hot tea, Officer Bradley arrived. He looked so normal in jeans, a sweatshirt, and a baseball cap. He welcomed me, shaking my hand in both of his and he sat across from me, beside his wife.

"First off," he said. "No more Officer Bradley. You can just call me Cooper."

"And I'm Emma."

"Ok," I replied, feeling right at home. "Thank you."

"How would you like to go about doing this?" he asked.

"Maybe I could interview you first."

"Sure," he said, "but you don't really have to ask me questions. Why don't I just tell you what happened from my point of view, which isn't that much really."

I only nodded in reply because my mouth was suddenly very dry. It was beginning to be too difficult to talk and I began to get emotional at the thought of finally hearing something about the death of my father. Emma moved around the table to sit beside me and she held my hands.

"I was just on patrol," Cooper started, "and a call came over the radio about the fire. Fire and ambulance had been dispatched. Witnesses calling in on 911 said someone was in a burning house. I was just hoping that the firemen would get there before it got too bad.

"I saw the flames from about three blocks away. When I turned the corner, there was a huge crowd. I had to ease the car through them to get up to the scene tape, and as I got out to check in with the policemen who were already on site, I saw a fireman running to the ambulance with what looked like a teenage girl in his arms. There were two other firemen running beside him. As they placed her in the care of the paramedics, the firemen leaned over her, listening. They looked back towards the house and in seconds, the ambulance departed the scene. The firemen returned to the house and fought the blaze for a long time. And when it was just smoke and smoldering ashes, they brought out a body and it was taken away. We took witness reports. There were two ladies that I spoke to. After you called, I visited them. They are both willing to talk to you although one has very little to tell and her story can be incorporated by the second. So, I told the second lady that we wanted to talk to her. She said she would be home all day. Are you up for that?"

I nodded through my tears and Emma gave me a hug.

"I'll take you there," Cooper said. "Then we will visit the firemen and I'll drop you off at your mother's office."

"Ok," was all I could manage.

As I turned off the tape recorder, I didn't know how I would cope with hearing everything to come. Sitting and listening to Cooper brought back the pain of that night so vividly. I just kept thinking that it was my daddy that he was talking about when he said they came out with a body. My father, with all of his humor, love, happiness, and caring reduced to being a body. I ached for him and for the fact that he died without me or Mummy at his side, whispering to him that we loved him more than he could ever know.

An hour or so later, we arrived at Mrs. Gardner's place. She was probably in her early eighties and she had an apartment in a retirement home in upper northwest Washington. She offered us tea, which we took. When she placed mine in front of me, she asked me to stand, and I did. Then she hugged me for some time and I took everything from that hug that she meant to give.

"Sit down, child," she said. "I will tell you what I know."

I started my tape recorder. Cooper and I waited quietly as she took a seat in her recliner.

"Two or three days a week, depending on how I'm feeling, I get on the bus and ride down to where your friend lived. I have a friend nearby who lives with her daughter and son-in-law. That day, I got off the bus just as a loud but dull boom startled me. When I looked towards the sound, I saw flames coming out of the basement windows of the house. I saw a silver SUV drive up. I believe it was a Honda," she said looking at Cooper.

"Yes, ma'am," he said. "It was."

Mrs. Gardner nodded and continued. "A young man got out of the car and he says, 'Oh my God, no!' Then a lady comes up to him and it seems like she knows him. She told him that a girl named Heidi was in the house. She said she had just talked to her five minutes ago. The young man became very agitated. Maybe uncomfortable is a better word. He was sweating and he kept wiping his hand over his mouth. It was like he was watching the end of the world and he was trying to figure out what he could do to stop it from happening.

"He said the name Heidi over and over, very quickly. He said it each time in almost a whisper. It was eerie, I must say. Then, he just started running. He ran past everybody and everything. People were yelling at him, 'Hey, don't go in there!' But he didn't even react to that. He just kept running, right on in through the front door. But he never came out again. I'm sorry, sweetheart. So sorry," she said looking at me.

He never came out again. Those words hit hard and I felt as if whenever I thought of him from that point on, all of my memories would end with the phrase "he never came out again."

"Thank you," I replied. "But please keep going. You can't know how much you are helping me and my mom."

She nodded and she smiled gently. "Well, there wasn't much more. We, all of us, did hear a loud scream. I think it was your friend, Heidi. We heard the name Eddie shouted. It was only once, but it was loud and clear. Not long after that, the young girl stumbled out of the house and fell on the ground. I think it was three firemen that went to her. One of them carried her to the ambulance. I couldn't watch anymore. So I walked a block, got on the next bus, and went home. I didn't sleep a bit that night. Not a bit."

The next thing I knew, Cooper was helping me up from my knees. I'd gone over to Mrs. Gardner's chair and laid my head on her lap and she had been brushing my hair.

In the car, Cooper asked if I had had enough. "We can do the firemen another day," he said.

"No," I replied, shaking my head. "I have to hear it all. I can't wait anymore. It's been too long already."

"Ok," he said. He grabbed my hand and gently squeezed it. "Let's do it."

When we pulled up to the fire station, I noticed a handmade sign stretched across the side of one of the hook and ladder trucks. It read, "Welcome Mae." I looked over at Cooper, who smiled back at me.

"Everyone cares," he said. "They really do."

I nodded and he patted my hand, which was beside me on the car seat, balled up in an intense fist. I relaxed beneath his touch and I realized that I was alone with a man for the first time since Daddy. There was so much that I missed.

We sat in the firehouse cafeteria. They made such a fuss over me, including making a pretty special lunch in my honor. While we ate, they took turns telling me about themselves and how they'd looked forward to this day since they got the phone call from Cooper.

"It's a kind of closure for us too," they said. "Most times we never get it. You can help us today as well."

After lunch, we got down to business and I started the tape recorder. Cooper was at my side and I felt really good about that. A fireman named Jake spoke first.

"I was first to move towards the house because I saw her first. She came out running. Her eyes were wide with fear. You know, you can only imagine the thoughts behind a look of fear like that. She stopped and turned back towards the house and then, she simply collapsed. I picked her up off the ground. It was getting extremely hot. Evan and Lucas got there just after me and we all turned to run her back to the paramedics. As we put her on the gurney, she grabbed my arm, Mae. She said to me, 'He fell. He fell to the basement. Eddie.'

By now, I was doing what I seemed to do a lot of in the last months. I don't think I even need to spell it out. They were so kind. They just paused while I got it all out. I so appreciated that gesture of kindness and patience. Cooper wrapped me up in his arms. Soon, when I became calmer, Evan picked up the story.

"I'm sorry, Mae, that we couldn't just rush into the house. There were too many flames and it was just too hot, you know?"

I nodded. "I understand."

"So we fought the fire until it was just smoldering ash basically. It was bad. By now I'm sure you know it was a boiler explosion."

Again, I nodded.

"But it was time. We knew someone was in there. A male named Eddie. And we knew he meant a lot to that little girl in the ambulance. At that time, we thought it was a friend. You know, maybe a boyfriend. Lucas suggested a brother. At any rate, we knew we had a job to do and we found him where the girl said we would. He had fallen into a separate room from the rest of the utility area."

"It was where Grace, Heidi's mom, did her ceramics," I added.

Evan nodded. "I'm sorry."

"It's ok. Thank you for going in after him."

"No problem," he continued. "We wouldn't have left him."

Jake spoke up again. "We did what we had to do then. We put him in a body bag and he was taken to the city morgue. And that's where we drop out of the story."

They all gave me hugs on the way back to the car. Through the car window, Jake handed me a patch with their firehouse number on it. They told me that I should visit them from time to time. They said how they would like that and I promised them that I would.

When we got into the car, I turned to Cooper and said, "I'm ready for my mom now. Really ready."

He smiled. "I bet. To say that it's been a very emotional day would be quite an understatement."

I agreed.

I waited in Mummy's office while she finished up for the day. She was anxious to listen to the tapes with me, but I told her that I couldn't handle that. I told her that she was on her own unless she wanted to give me a couple of days to get it together. She couldn't wait and I can certainly understand why. So after dinner, we split. Mummy went to her bedroom to listen to the audiotapes and I went to the basement and put in a videotape. I was four or five years old in this one and we were on Edward's Island, Maine, where Grammy and Grandpa had a house. Mummy and Daddy had friends up for the weekend. Daddy, the guy friend whose name is never mentioned, and I, were on Big Beach. I had played myself into complete exhaustion. The camera had been running the whole time I played. I'd been digging waterways and building castles. From time to time, I ran off with another kid to splash in the water and the camera kept running. I must say that I was kind of cute.

But as I said, I soon ran out of gas and I flopped down in Daddy's lap. He did something that he did often, which was to forget to turn the camera off. There was plenty of wasted time on many tapes due to his forgetfulness. This time, I'd fallen asleep on Daddy's lap and the camera showed my feet lying across his legs, which were pointing out towards the water.

I lay back on the floor and stared at the ceiling. I thought about Mummy upstairs listening to the audio tapes from earlier in the day. I was feeling guilty about putting her through it alone since I'd had Cooper with me. But I just couldn't do it, and I became distracted anyway by the conversation happening on the videotape.

> Guy Friend: Did you hear about that pro football player that died trying to save his cat's life?
>
> Daddy: I read something about it.
>
> Guy Friend: Man, you really have to love your cat. (laughing)
>
> Daddy: I guess.
>
> Guy Friend: Would you do that? Sacrifice yourself for an animal?
>
> Daddy: (a chuckle) I doubt it.
>
> Guy Friend: (after a short break in the conversation) Let's up the ante? Who or what would you sacrifice yourself for?

Daddy: Where is this going? I hate hypotheticals.

Guy Friend: I'm just curious. That's all.

Daddy: I'd sacrifice myself for my wife and child without thinking about it. That good enough?

Guy Friend: (laughs) No. Too easy. Listen, man, I love my life and I can't really think of a situation that would cause me to put it in jeopardy for someone else. I have a wife. I have a teenage son. I can't think of anything that would make me take a chance on losing them or putting them through the grief of losing me.

By now, I was sitting up and staring at the television not believing the conversation that I was hearing.

Daddy: I can't imagine a situation like that either, because I obviously have a daughter and a wife and I also kind of love living. But I don't know if I can say "never ever."

Guy Friend: Absolutely, I can.

Daddy: What about if you were witnessing or about to witness a rape?

Guy Friend: Hypothetical!

Daddy: You started this.

Guy Friend: Ok, cell phone and 911.

Daddy: And you could stand there and watch it happen until they get there?

Guy Friend: Well, if a guy is doing that he probably has a knife or a gun and I'm no fighter. I think the phone call is the best I could do.

Daddy: I don't think I could just stand there.

Guy Friend: So you would risk everything?

Daddy: Truthfully, how could I not help? And who would I be if I didn't? What kind of man would my wife and daughter think I was if I just stood by and watched something like that. Even if I'd already called 911. Even more, I couldn't live with myself. I'd be haunted the rest of my life by something like that. I wouldn't *want* to live like that. I could see myself changing into something that no one could live with, much less me. I couldn't face myself and I couldn't face my wife and daughter ever. I would be a dead man walking.

Guy Friend: Wow. That's deep.

Daddy: Well, you asked. I think I'd rather be dead and have them be proud of me for trying to do what's right rather than wake up every morning to look at my wife and feel her disgust for me.

"Mummy!" I screamed. "Mummy!"

I ran for the stairs, calling for her. I burst through her bedroom door. Later, she would describe me as "tearfully ecstatic" and I suppose that I was. She had been lying on the bed, her eyes already red from listening to what I had recorded earlier in the day.

"You have to come," I shouted.

"What is it?"

"You have to come. It's Daddy. It's the answer, Mummy. It's the answer we have been waiting for."

She looked stunned and maybe a little confused. Daddy was dead after all. How could he be providing me with answers? Maybe she thought I'd finally gone over the edge. At any rate, she hadn't moved so I grabbed her by the arm and pulled her off the bed. "You have to hear it for yourself," I said as I continued to tug at her. Once I got her downstairs, I rewound the tape.

"Just listen," I said, breathlessly. "Just sit and listen."

When it was over, we just sat there in stunned and silent relief. From beyond, Daddy had set us free. We played it over and over again and laughed and cried and hugged until, from exhaustion, we fell asleep on the basement floor. When we woke up the next morning, we played it again. Then we put the phone next to the speaker of the television and played it for Gran Gran and Pop Pop. "My Lord," Gran Gran said to me. "Oh, my Lord."

And finally, we played it for Grammy and Grandpa.

"You must be so very proud of him, Mae," Grammy said.

"Oh, I am," I replied. "No daughter could ever be more proud. And that's the whole truth and nothing but the truth."

ELEVEN

Mummy had asked me to call Heidi right after we finished playing the tape to family members, but I chose not to. I figured that after all that had come to pass, I would only be allowed to see her with Ethan and Grace present. This was between the two of us and I needed to settle it that way, face to face. She would be on her own at school and it would be easier for me to pull her into a quiet corner or an empty classroom. At least that was the plan.

So the first day after Christmas break, I walked into school on a mission of forgiveness. Not that I was preparing to offer it mind you, but rather to ask for it. For the first time in a long while, I was actually seeking Heidi Foster. And wouldn't you know it? She was nowhere to be found.

So I went to classes, hearing Daddy's words from the videotape echo in my head and also feeling very guilty and quite ashamed. It all added up to me not being able to concentrate at all. My history teacher, Mr. Avidon, walked by my desk and put his hand on my shoulder. He didn't say anything. He just smiled when I reacted to his touch.

He knew that I was off somewhere, but he also knew that I needed to be there and he just wanted me to know that it was ok. It was over-the-top thoughtful and I will never forget him for that gift.

Later, while walking down the stairs into the student forum where the school gathers for lunch, I saw Heidi. She was coming into the forum from the outside and I realized she had just come to school. There she was standing at the bottom of the stairs, looking very much the loner, but somehow less troubled than before the holiday, although still not the Heidi I used to know. A change caused by the fire and which I had added to over and over again. With that thought I was overwhelmed really. Everything came flooding back to me, but interestingly enough, I was comfortable with it all except for the way I had been treating Heidi.

I marched through the crowd and down the stairs, amongst most of the student body eating their lunches, playing guitar, chatting, and napping. I marched right up to Heidi and took her hands in mine, all the while hoping that she wouldn't push me away or slap me across my face. Without having to look, I first heard silence around me and then whispers. But I needed to tune all of that out. I just wanted to look into the eyes of my friend. My old friend Heidi Foster.

She'd watched me come down the stairs toward her and her expression slowly began to change. If she had been feeling together, she was now beginning to lose it. She began to show signs of vulnerability the closer I came to her. Later she would tell me that she knew I hated her, and she began to fear that this was the moment of reckoning that had been hovering like a disturbing premonition. She felt that this was finally "it" and she thought how sad it was that this collision was about to take place in front of the whole school. She decided that she would not fight back. She had decided to offer herself up to me, to let me strike out with abandon. And then, maybe she would feel she had given all she could to me and be satisfied. And that maybe I would see this and forgive or just finally lift the veil of hatred with which I had covered her.

When I took her hands in mine, Heidi started to cry and she began to shake.

"I'm so sorry," she said, but I put my fingers to her lips to quiet her.

"No. No you don't," I said. "I never want to hear you say that again. It was me, Heidi. It was me. I am so, so ashamed and I will never forgive myself for the way I've hurt you."

Heidi was surprised and through her tears, I felt my friend begin to come back to me and I could not handle that and so I joined her in tears. We hugged each other as if it were the last hug ever to be given. I felt myself going limp and Heidi held me up for a second, but then we both just let go. We sat on the floor in the student forum just rocking each other in that big, big hug. Before long, I felt arms around us and when I opened my eyes, I saw a very blurry Mr. Barr looking down on me.

"How I have waited for this day," he said, smiling.

He lifted us and said, "Let's go to my office where you can have some privacy. No more school for you two today."

As we walked up the stairs, kids reached out and touched us. Our old friends Ellie, Zoe, Carol, Charlotte, Maria, Paige came running and they stopped us for hugs like we were a newly married couple walking through a line of well-wishers at their wedding. I could only say that I was sorry. I kept saying it over and over again. But I was lucky, wasn't I? Friends have this thing about forgiving and I got a lot of that forgiveness on the way to Mr. Barr's office.

In the office, I set about trying to make things right. I explained again that I was so very sorry. That I had been blinded by my loss and a hatred that I never knew existed inside of me.

"And now that I know — had I really, really been clear-headed enough to think about it — I would have known then. It should have been so easy to see, knowing my father," I said.

"What do you mean? Had you known what?"

"Oh," I said, chuckling. "I'm getting ahead of myself. I will show you what helped me. I think that maybe it will help you too."

Heidi's eyes were still watery and so were mine. I reached into my backpack, which Mr. Barr had carried into his office. I pulled out a tissue pack and noticed the tape recorder and smiled. This was exactly the way to end my research if she would be willing. I pulled it and the tissues out and handed the tissue pack to Heidi. As she wiped her eyes and blew her nose, I explained my earlier day of discovery. I told her about Cooper, Emma, Mrs. Gardner, and the firemen. I asked for permission to hear and to record her story and she granted it.

"I would be happy to tell you," she replied.

I sensed that she needed to tell it. I sensed that this had been as much a burden for her as my misplaced hatred. I knew that if I wanted to help smooth the waters that I had troubled, I had to hear from Heidi what it had been like for her. So I sat beside her on the couch in Mr. Barr's office and prepared myself to hear a very different tale from my own. It would be my penance. The first of many steps toward healing.

"The moment I woke up in the hospital," Heidi said, "I knew that everything had changed forever. I felt it in my soul and I saw it so strongly in the eyes of my parents. I was afraid to look in a mirror because I was afraid of how that truth would look on my own face. The thought of it terrified me. I thought of Eddie constantly. I saw the last frame. You know the photo that your brain takes? I saw it constantly. It crushed me constantly. Mom, Dad, and Gina offered me love and understanding but I couldn't accept it. I was hollow and unable to respond. It's hard for me to say what it really felt like. It was a dull feeling and it was heavy. When I lay on my back, it always felt like someone was lying on top of me, squeezing my breath away.

"Then at some point, I thought of you. I'm sorry that I didn't right away. There was only Eddie, my grief, and my guilt. But when I remembered you, it was like a mother who's misplaced a child in the department store, you know?

I had to find you right away, or else. I had to hold you and make sure you were all right. But then, Mom told me that you didn't want to see me. I was devastated.

"Then they took me home, which, of course, was not really home. It's the rented apartment we are still in. The next day Mom tried to gently tell me that we were not going to Eddie's funeral. She said that Renata had called to say that you didn't want me there and that you were, should I say, quite passionate about it. She told me that you blamed me for his death. 'You're too late, Mae,' I thought. 'I already blame me enough for the both of us.'

"But as the days went by, I still held out hope that you would see me. I still believed that we had shared so much. We knew each other's hearts so well. 'She has to come around,' I thought. 'She has to.' But when you wouldn't, a very sad reality set in. The reality that I'd lost two people who I had loved and that it was my fault for getting into this mess in the first place. I kept thinking, 'If I only hadn't been listening to music. Maybe I would have heard something. Maybe this would have never happened.' But it had happened.

"At this point, I began reeling. I lost my center and things just began to come apart. I wanted to see you and to tell you how sorry I was. I wanted to say 'thank you' to Eddie and to whisper to him at his service that I understood that every day I lived from this point on was a gift from him. But I couldn't. It all just remained bottled up inside me. And it began to eat at me. It hurt so much that I tried to shut off that part of me, you know? The funny thing is, I figured out how to do it and pretty soon I stopped hurting, but I just felt even emptier. Then the emptiness began to hurt. It's true. It's the weirdest thing.

"Mom had some of our friends come over in an attempt to help me out.

"They did all of the talking. I just sat there. They said that none of them had been to see you because Renata had been telling people that you weren't ready yet. But they convinced me, or I wanted to be convinced, that school would fix it all. There was all this excitement about being at the high school. 'Once you were back in the school environment,' they said, 'things would get better quickly.' They made a big deal out of preparing a big greeting for us on the first day of school. But we know how that worked out.

"And later, when I saw the anger in your eyes and the hatred in the set of your face, I began to fall away to somewhere I never knew existed. It is a terrible place and I have been there all this time, waiting for you. Waiting to tell you that I'm sorry I didn't get out on my own. I didn't think it was possible. There was fire everywhere. I just went into the closet because there was no place else to go. I felt it was over, my life. I guess the impulse to live is what drove me in there. To survive for just a few more minutes, you know?

"I couldn't just stand there and let it burn me. I guess it was sort of like chess. I had to move to the last possible square of safety.

"Minutes before that though, it was the same old life. I came home and read the note from Mom that said that she and Gina were at the grocery store. I went outside to put a letter in the corner mailbox and said a few words to our neighbor, Mrs. Stein. I had been listening to Ben Folds on my iPod before I spoke to her and as I went back inside, I put my ear buds in.

"So I was upstairs in the quiet of my room. I liked it that way every once in a while. Having the whole house to myself. I was happy. I remember that. I felt very happy. I was even smiling when I saw the flames come rushing in.

"Everyone says there was an explosion, but I never heard or felt anything. One moment everything was normal, you know? The next moment, I felt heat. I turned around and flames rolled into my room like….like water really. It was fluid. It took my bed first and from there the curtains and then the window. There was a fire escape ladder under my bed. Wouldn't you know it?

"In no time at all, the handwriting was on the wall for me. Flames in the doorway, flames in the window, and flames overtaking my bathroom. All that was left was me, my desk, and the closet. Still, I had time to think it through. I saw my life, Mom, Dad, Gina, and everything else moving away from me and I just couldn't believe it. I knew that I was going to die and I knew it was going to be painful. Already my skin felt like it was on fire. At that point, instinct took over and I shut myself in the closet. It got hotter and I just rocked back and forth and waited. I began to cry. Just seconds before, I had been singing and smiling. Just seconds before, I thought I was going to live for a very long time.

"Then there was the sweetest sound ever. It was my name. Someone was screaming Heidi. I heard these bursts of air and then the closet door opened. And there he was, Mae. Flames all around him. He'd found both of our fire extinguishers and he'd put out the fire around the closet door. And somehow he'd wet Gina's mattress. It lay like a soggy bridge over the threshold. He held out his hand to me. 'Let's go, Heidi,' he said to me. 'We've got to go now.'

"But I was frozen with fear and he could see that. He grabbed my arm with his free hand and lifted me out of the closet. Fire had taken over the doorway to the hall again. He sprayed it with the extinguisher and pulled me through and we turned to run down the hallway towards the staircase, which was on fire but still there. And then it happened."

Heidi stopped. She was crying and she looked at me. I was crying. This was the moment I had been waiting for since the night we first met Cooper Bradley. Since that night when we went to bed with cold food still on the kitchen table and bad news on our hearts.

Heidi was waiting and I understood. "I'm ready," I said. "I'm ready to hear it."

She slid next to me and wrapped me in her arms. She spoke softly, next to my ear.

"He was in front of me and the floor…it just fell away and he fell through the opening, but he caught himself. He was holding himself up with his elbows and the back of his arms and he started to yell because he was getting burned. I tried to pull him up, but I couldn't lift him and he didn't have the strength. But he tried again to push himself up and out of the hole, but more of it gave way and he was hanging only by his hands. He yelled to me, 'Get the fire extinguisher. Spray your way down the stairs.' I said, 'No.' I told him that I couldn't leave him. He'd just saved my life. But he kept telling me and then he stopped speaking. There was fear in his eyes and an incredible sadness. He was emotionally where I had been no more than two minutes ago, but I knew and he knew that I could not save him. He yelled. 'Run, Heidi. Run.'

"And then he was gone and I just screamed his name. I grabbed the extinguisher and slid around the hole and I saw him on the basement floor and he wasn't moving. But I did as he said. I sprayed everything in front of me and found my way outside where I collapsed. A fireman picked me up. I remember the doors of the ambulance closing and then nothing until I woke up in the hospital and into this nightmare.

"That's how it happened, Mae. That's everything. I hope it helps you to know this, because I want to do whatever I can to ease whatever I can. I will forever be thankful and I will always work to honor the gift he has given me."

"Oh, Heidi," I said. "I know you will. You have been all along. I'm so sorry that I got in the way."

Heidi pulled back from our embrace and I smiled at her because this time, there was no more room for anger and I did not want to look through her. I wanted to see everything about her.

I don't know how long we had been sitting there, staring quietly at each other, when the door opened and Mummy stepped inside. She saw surprise on our faces.

"Mr. Barr called," she said. "I just wanted to be here, so I left work. I want to take you both home with me. Grace says it's ok, Heidi. If you want to that is."

"I do," Heidi replied. "I do."

When we got home, I gave Mummy Heidi's audiotape and I told her that this time I would listen with her, but she said, "No," with a smile. She said she wanted to listen to this alone. I understood.

"Take Heidi downstairs," she said. "Play the videotape for her."

"I will," I said. "I can't wait to show it to her."

And I did play it for her and it turned out to be just as comforting for her as it had been for Mummy and me. For me, it released my anger towards everyone, but especially Daddy. It answered the question "why" and left me with nothing but the pride he hoped we would feel. For Heidi, it took away the guilt because what he did that day was as much for him, Mummy, and me as it was for her. It had not been her responsibility.

Heidi spent the night at our house and like old times, we talked deep into the night.

TWELVE

Lately, my dreams are of rose petals drifting on the water. The river's surface is glistening as it meets the late morning sun. It is inviting and I respond, diving from some perch that I cannot see, diving through the rose petals until I am engulfed by the water and its warmth. Beneath the surface, the sunlight illuminates everything around me and soon, into the light, comes my father. He floats at a distance and he smiles. He is happy and he wants the same for me. I feel it. I smile back as he reaches for me and I reach for him. I should be touching his hand, but I can't. It moves through mine, but it leaves a rumbling inside of me that subsides with a ripple effect that moves throughout my body. Daddy waves good-bye and he mouths the words, "Be happy."

This dream is my dream. I have never spoken of it, not even to Mummy because it is mine alone. Each night, I go to bed hoping to see my father and when I do, I rise to meet the day with incredible joy. I am happy.

But there are some things that still make me sad, like marking important days that belonged to Daddy and me. Days like Father's Day. On the first one after his death, I had nothing planned. Mummy never even mentioned that the day was approaching. I think we both hoped it would miss us like a bad weather system that passes just a little to the north. But Father's Day came anyway and I awakened feeling a little sad and I immediately sought to distract myself. Within minutes, still in my pajamas, I was on the couch watching a new tennis phenom, Rafael Nadal, play tennis. Daddy never got me to play the game, but I did learn to appreciate it.

So I was startled when the doorbell rang. I shuffled off to answer it and I found Ethan Foster standing at our door. I let him in with a smile.

"Happy Father's Day," he said.

"Oh," I said, with a sigh, my hand to my heart. "You're so sweet."

"Well, that goes without saying."

I laughed. "And modest too."

"You're two for two."

I laughed again. "Come into the family room," I said. "I was just watching some tennis. Would you like something to drink?"

Mummy came down to greet Ethan and they shared a laugh as well. And when they were done, he turned to me.

"Well, it's Father's Day, Mae."

"Yeah, you said that already."

"I did and I am waiting for you to get dressed."

Now I just stood with my mouth hanging open.

"I'm here to take you to brunch, silly. That's usually how it goes on Father's Day, you know? The daughter takes the father to brunch and the father pays. You remember that, right?"

Mummy and I roared with laughter.

"Yes," I said. "I remember it well."

I walked over to Ethan Foster and gave him a huge hug and told him that I would take a quick shower and be right back. Mummy kept him company. For the next three years, he took me to brunch on Father's Day. And he was in my life all the time. He helped me with homework. He took me to the action movies that Daddy and I liked and Heidi hated. He brought a consistent male voice into my life, a voice that sounded always like love.

On that day, I also received flowers from Cooper Bradley and the firefighters, Jake, Evan, and Lucas. They'd gotten together and had their picture taken and today it sits by my bed, next to the one of Mummy and me on Santa's lap. Cooper's little daughter, Doris, also became a good friend of mine. I babysat for her until I went off to college.

As for Heidi and me, we remain the very, very best of friends. Although we do remember my father together in many ways, we do not speak of the fire itself very often. Or of the trauma that followed. We have learned to have it be a part of who we are without letting it overwhelm us.

In the days that followed our reconciliation, we fell quickly back into our large group of friends. We became normal kids again. I played volleyball and Heidi ran cross country. We went to dances, tried out for the school musicals, and fought over dating Brandon Bell. Our high school years were good years and through all of it we were inseparable. When asked to describe our friendship, our buddy Charlotte responded by saying, "Find Heidi and you find Mae. Or vice versa!"

Enough said.

About The Author

JEFFREY BLOUNT is an Emmy Award-winning television director and an award recipient for scriptwriting on multiple documentary projects. Born and raised in rural Virginia, he now lives in Washington, DC, with his wife, Jeanne Meserve. They have two children, Julia and Jake.

Made in the USA
San Bernardino, CA
06 July 2020